What kids say about *Left Out*...

"It deals with real life problems that aren't just about having a crush on a boy or losing a good luck charm."

–Kathleen, 12

"This is a fabulous book. It is one of the rare sports books that also has real life problems and conflicts away from the field. Read *Left Out!*"

–Matt, 12

"The author portrays girls in a more confident, self-assured way than what has been done by other authors."

–Nora, 12

"I think it was one of the best books I've read. It was unbelievably real and a great story."

–Matt, 12

"It is fun to read whether you are a sports fan or not."

–Cristina, 12

W9-BIX-758

Other books by **The Broadway Ballplayers**™

LEFT
OUT
by Rosie

Series by
Maureen Holohan

For information regarding permission, please write to:

The Broadway Ballplayers, Inc.
P.O. Box 597
Wilmette, IL 60091
(847)-570-4715

ISBN: 0-9659091-1-5

*This book is dedicated
to those who allow
their actions to speak.*

You are strong.

Chapter One

You know what everybody says about people who don't talk much.

"She's stuck-up."

"She doesn't like anybody."

"She's boring."

The one I heard the most was: "All she cares about is baseball."

I couldn't help but wonder how others could talk so much about a person they never even tried to get to know.

My mother told me once that shy people will always see what people who are too busy talking will always miss. She was right. I saw a lot pass before my eyes when no one knew I was watching. Here's a story I will never forget.

• • • •

The red light turned on as the next ball dropped into the machine's long, steel grip. After a slow wind up, the arm flung itself in the direction of home plate. It was there that my brother Rico stood waiting to hammer it away. With one powerful step, and a quick twist of his shoulders, the fat of his bat drilled the white blur into the drooping net above. As the ball fell dead to the dirt, Rico quickly returned to his stance. Not even three seconds passed before the light flicked on again, which indicated the delivery of another fiery fastball.

Nothing held my attention more than the speed of a baseball. I watched my brother's eyes take the 90 mile-per-hour pitches virtually to a complete stop in midair before he blasted them away. He cracked hits right, left, and straight down the middle. Hardly any passed him by.

"Just one more," he muttered.

Rico always ended his workout with a sure connection that he could easily judge the distance on — even in a batting cage. A hit that on a bright blue-skied day would sail its way over a crowd and clear out of a ballpark. This was the blast that allowed him to sleep that night, and dream about getting another shot at returning to the sport that had become so much a part of the both of us.

Of course, this took time. Rico got a hold of a few solid ones, but they weren't good enough. I sat there wondering how long it would take before he rested. Five minutes passed. Then ten. *Come on, Rico!* On the next pitch, I heard the sound. A loud and solid *crack* hung in the air. That was it. Rico dropped the bat off his shoulder, and took a deep breath. He turned his squinting eyes toward me and said, "Your turn, kid."

I jumped up from my spot on the bench and hurried into the cage. My brother grabbed his dirty baseball cap off a hook, and slipped it backwards on his head. He strutted down to the machine and adjusted its speed.

"What's it on?" I asked.

"Fifty," he yelled.

Fifty? I was tired of hitting the slow ones. I wanted speed. Smoke. The heat. I slid my helmet on and then tightened my batting glove. "Put it on seventy," I said confidently.

Rico smiled as he shook his head. "The wind might knock you over."

"Please just one try?"

"It's only going to hurt your form if you try swinging at pitches you're not ready for," he warned.

"Sixty-five?"

He didn't answer me. I looked at him with heavy, little-sister eyes. Rico huffed, shook his head and walked back to the machine. He turned the dial.

Adrenaline rushed through me. I gripped the taped handle of the bat firmly and held my breath. My eyes grew wide as the arm rose. It snapped back and then flung forward. The ball hissed and I swung hard. *Thump.* The ball smacked solidly against the padded backstop. I took a deep breath and unwound myself slowly.

"You sure are fearless," Rico said with a grin.

Thump. Another ball flew past me. I eyed the machine, and grunted as I swung wildly at the next. *Thump.* In a fury I returned to my stance, determined to knock the stitches out of the next piece of leather that flew by my face. But I didn't have another chance. I watched helplessly as Rico turned the dial back to where he had first placed it.

"Stubborn," I mumbled as I dropped my bat.

"You say somethin'?" he yelled back.

I shook my head.

"Hit away, kid," he called out.

I tapped my bat on home plate twice and lined myself up in the batting box. I cracked the first, and then the next. Rico watched silently as I warmed up some more. After a dozen pitches, I heard the familiar rumble of a lawn mower. I looked up from under my oversized helmet and smiled. Dressed in his jeans, dark sunglasses, and royal blue baseball cap, Mr. Baker rode up to the fence and shut off his mower.

"How's everybody hittin' this afternoon?" Mr. Baker asked.

"Not bad," Rico answered with a smile.

Rico had started coming to Mr. Baker's cages when he was in grade school. He saved up his allowance money every week and rode his bike three miles each way. Mr. Baker told me one story about my brother back when he was in the eighth grade. After striking out three times in one game, Rico could barely sleep. At dawn he crawled out of bed, jumped on his bike, rode through the city, and waited on Mr. Baker's steps until he came out to pick up the morning paper. When he stepped outside, Rico asked Mr. Baker if he would let him in the cages so he could hit before school started. Mr. Baker said he'd never seen a kid work so hard, and care so much, so he offered my brother a deal. If Rico gave Mr. Baker's tractors and cars regular washes, Rico could use the cages for free. Rico was so happy that he washed Mr. Baker's cars three times that week.

"She has a good eye there," Mr. Baker said as I cracked another.

"Yeah," Rico said. "Nice hit, kid."

"She's playing with the city all-stars for the state championships this month, right?" Mr. Baker asked.

"We don't know yet," Rico said softly.

"They'd be crazy not to take her," Mr. Baker said. "I've been watching baseball for a long, long time, and she's special."

"I know," Rico said quietly. He intentionally lowered his voice so I wouldn't be able to hear what they were talking about. But I heard every word.

"They've never had a girl on the team before," Rico explained, "and some people don't think it's a good idea."

I took myself out of the conversation and focused my eyes and ears solely on the machine and its humming racket. I didn't want to hear about what everyone else thought anymore. I didn't care if folks were up in arms either for me or against me. I swung harder and faster, pounding one ball and then snapping my bat back for the next. All I wanted to do was play, just like any other player in the city.

"Go get 'em, kid," Mr. Baker yelled to me before he fired up his mower again. I tipped my helmet up and smiled in return. Then I quickly turned my attention back to the mechanical arm, swung and foul tipped one over my head.

"You dipped your shoulder," Rico said. "Don't lift your head off the ball. Just meet it. Come on, kid. Hammer this one away."

Rico stayed with me on every pitch. He encouraged me on the good ones, and called out all the adjustments I needed after not getting a hold of the others. I blasted one last shot.

"We're outta here," Rico said.

I wanted to stay. But just before I started complaining about it, I took a long look at my brother's glum face.

"You gotta game tonight, Ric?" I asked.

"No," he muttered. "Tomorrow night."

"You hear anything from your agent?" I asked.

When he shook his head, my heart sank. I felt awful for asking. I walked over and helped him straighten up the bats and helmets in the cage. We headed over to his midnight blue Mustang in silence, and dumped our gear in the trunk.

"Thirsty?" Rico asked, and I nodded my head.

We both jogged across the street to the corner store. After we bought two tall glasses of lemonade, we headed back to his car.

"I'll be at your game on Saturday," he assured me.

With a record of eight wins and nine losses, we didn't have a chance at making the playoffs, which made the next game our last of the regular season. I could keep playing only if I were chosen for the all-star team.

"When do you find out?" Rico asked.

"After the game," I replied.

"Are you nervous?" he asked.

I dropped my head and shrugged my shoulders. I could feel my brother's eyes on me as he stared from across the roof of his car.

"Whatever they decide, you and I both know what you deserve," he said. "Right?"

I dropped my head down and wished everyone would stop bringing it up. I was not going to talk about it.

"You okay, kid?" Rico asked.

"Can you drop me off at the park?" I asked.

I opened the car door and slid inside so Rico wouldn't ask me any more questions. It annoyed him when I didn't talk about things. He was afraid that holding all my thoughts inside wasn't good for me. But what he didn't know was that I talked to him more than to anyone else. Just being with him made most of my worries go away.

• • • •

We cruised down Broadway Ave. and I looked into the doorways and windows of my friends' houses. No one was in sight, which meant they were all at our favorite hangout. Rico stopped at the corner of Woodside and Broadway, which was the home of Anderson Park.

"Don't be too long," he yelled to me as I jumped out of the car. "You've got to get some dinner before practice tonight."

"I know," I mumbled. Before I slammed the door shut, I flipped my cap backwards just like my brother. Rico smiled as he added, "Be good, kid."

I clenched my ball tight in my mitt, and started running. I weaved around the kids on the playground, skipped over the basketball courts and headed right to the sandlot where all of my friends were getting ready for a game of 500.

"J.J.'s up and Penny pitches first," Molly shouted. She turned her freckled face toward me. "Hey, Rosie. Where ya been?"

"At the cages with Rico."

Wil wiped the dripping water from her face as she jogged back from the water fountain. "Hey, Rosie," she asked, "you hear about the all-star team yet?"

I wanted to scream. "No," I mumbled.

Penny eyed me suspiciously. "When do you find out?" she asked.

"Saturday."

"They better put you on it," Angel said.

"Yeah," Wil breathed deeply when she came to a halt. "Tell them they'll have to deal with me and Molly and the rest of the Ballplayers here if they don't," she said sternly. Then she sighed before cracking a smile. "And trust me — they don't want to deal with us."

"I'd be scared if I were them," Penny said with a smile.

I felt a slight bit of relief, knowing I had my friends behind me.

"Let's play ball!" Molly called out.

Wil tripped as she jogged out onto the field, and she glanced around in a panic hoping nobody saw her. Her eyes met mine and I laughed. I always laughed at Wil. We were complete opposites. She was tall. I was short. She talked all the time. I didn't talk much at all except when I was around my brother.

"You don't mess with the Ballplayers," Wil yelled smiling.

I grinned as I skipped onto the field with my friends. I repeated our new group nickname to my-self in my mind. *The Ballplayers.* I liked it.

Up until that summer, most of the people on the North Side of the city just called us "The Kids from Broadway." That all changed in early June when our neighborhood team played in the city summer bas-ketball league. When we were asked our team name, together we decided that it would only be proper to call us simply by where we came from and what we were. Taking into consideration that we all lived on the same street — Broadway Avenue — and that we played any and every sport, only one name seemed to suit us all. From then on, we were known as *The Broadway Ballplayers.*

"Are you gonna pitch before sundown, P, or what?" Jeffrey "J.J." Jasper shouted at Penny.

Penny, who was dressed in her matching purple sweatbands, white T-shirt, and baggy black shorts, always stayed as cool as she looked. She took her time finishing what she had to say, and then lobbed J.J. the ball. He drilled a grounder toward Wil. It bounced up and hit her in the shoulder.

"Ow!" she yelped, and she tumbled over. Everybody knew Wil wasn't hurt. The only thing that she injured was her pride after she missed her chance at 50 points.

"That thing you have in your hand is called a mitt," J.J. shouted. "Maybe you should try and use it when that little white thing comes flying at you next time."

Wil looked up at him and scowled. She picked up the ball and gunned it back to J.J.

"Just get your body in front of it," Angel said patiently.

"I did that," Wil yelled. "It hit my body and it hurt!"

There was no such thing as sympathy at the park. If you didn't know how to play, you would have to either learn fast or not play at all. And even if you tried your best and you made a bad play, you still heard about it. If I were in the distance, I would probably have been laughing quietly at Wil too. But I was standing right next to her on this play and I could see how much it hurt. Wil smacked the ground with her mitt and everyone burst into laughter again. Except for having a tough time with grounders, Wil was a decent player. She needed somebody. I walked over to her and said quietly, "You okay, Wil?"

"Yeah," she mumbled. She grunted as she pulled herself up and re-adjusted her glasses. "I'm all right. You've really got to work with me, Rosie. I can't get those grounders."

"Should we put you back on the injured reserve list?" J.J. shouted.

"I'm fine," Wil said firmly. "Go ahead, hit me another one."

J.J. slammed another hit right at her. Wil ran up to it, bent over and it went right between her legs. The laughter continued. Even Penny, who was always fair to everyone at the park, scooped her hand over her mouth.

"You want another one, Wil?" shouted Eddie, the neighborhood bully. "I'm having fun just watching you."

"Shut up, Eddie," Wil said.

I didn't know what to say. "Don't listen to him," I finally mumbled.

It didn't help, but I couldn't think of anything else. Wil stood there with her right hand on her hip, and her lips pursed. "I wasn't ready," she muttered as she looked at the ground.

J.J. drilled his next shot at me. I made a clean scoop and zipped a hard throw back to Penny.

"Oh, sure, thanks a lot," Wil said. "Make me look bad."

I hated when I wanted to talk and nothing came out. I just shrugged my shoulders and remained silent.

"And don't give me that 'I-just-can't-help-it' look," she added, trying to sound tough. She looked at me and shook her head. "Say something please?"

I shrugged again.

"Ugh!" Wil threw her arms up in the air help-lessly. She eyed me again hoping I would speak. I put my mitt over my mouth and giggled. Wil's straight face broke into a wide grin.

I exhaled. What a relief it was to finally see her smile.

Chapter Two

L ater that evening I heard a familiar rap on our front door as I was sitting at the kitchen table. I gulped down what was left in my glass of milk and yelled, "Come on in, Sleep!"

With a pearly white smile, my best friend walked into the kitchen.

"Hey Rosie," he said. "What 'cha been doing?"

"Playing 500 at the park. I thought you'd be there. Where were ya?"

"I just got back from my grandma's," he said as he turned his baseball cap backwards just like mine and just like Rico's.

"My mom will be home any minute to take us to practice," I said. "You want half?" I reached out and offered him my sandwich.

He shook his head. "I already ate. Where's Rico?"

"He's probably out with what's-her-name," I mumbled. "We went to the cages today."

"You did?" he gasped.

"I tried calling you, but you weren't home."

Sleepy's hazel, weary eyes filled with disappointment. It was at these moments especially when one could see why my best friend, Scotty Jackson, was nicknamed Sleepy.

"Rico's coming to the game on Saturday," I said to lift his spirits. "He said to let you know that the bet's still on. One milkshake for every homer you hit."

Sleepy's grin was so wide it almost touched both ears.

"How many do you have this season?" I asked.

"Seven," he replied. "I think I can get two or three Saturday."

"You'll have a whole summer's worth of milkshakes if Rico keeps the bet when you make the all-star team."

The second the words came out of my mouth, I knew they should have remained as thoughts in my mind. I always felt comfortable around my best friend, but neither of us liked to talk about making the all-star team. A few silent, awkward seconds passed before I changed the subject.

"Let's go wait for my mom," I said.

We grabbed our mitts and headed out to the porch. Within a few minutes, our dark green station wagon pulled into the driveway.

"Hi, Rosa," my mother said. My name rolled off her tongue with a slight Puerto Rican accent. She gave me a kiss.

I wiped her lipstick off my cheek. "Hi, Mama," I said.

"And hi, Scotty. *¿Cómo estás?*"

"*Bien,*" he responded and he smiled proudly. "*¿Cómo está usted?*"

My mother went on about her day, talking in Spanish. She spoke too fast for Sleepy to understand. He raised one eyebrow as he listened. When she stopped Sleepy said, "I didn't get it all. What'd she say, Rosie?" My mother and I looked at him and laughed.

The drive to Tucker Park took only 15 minutes. My mother pulled into the parking lot and stopped the car.

"Your father will come by after work to pick you up," she said as I opened the door. "Have fun, Rosa, and you too, Scotty! Let them know who you are, and don't let 'em ever forget it! *¡Arriba, arriba!*"

"*¡Arriba, arriba!*" Sleepy repeated.

I rolled my eyes at my friend, and hurried out of the car. If I didn't hustle, my mother would have kept going on and on. She always made sporty cheers up as she went along, and ended up stringing together ideas that didn't make a whole lot of sense. It was all very embarrassing for me. Just before I slammed the car door shut, she shouted, "Hammer away!" That was easily her all-time favorite cheer. She abbreviated it from one of her favorite Puerto Rican proverbs that was hung on our living room wall: "Pray to God and hammer away!" I looked at Sleepy again and shook my head. He laughed as we jogged onto the field.

"Hey!" called out our coach, Mr. Martino. "Are you two hot dogs ready to play tonight or what?"

"Yep," Sleep hollered as he scooped up a ball.

"Today we're scrimmaging," Mr. Martino announced as the rest of the team streamed on the field for warm-ups. We all cheered. "Coaches are in, too."

"Can I be captain?" our first baseman asked.

I never begged to be captain. Even though I loved having my team stacked with the best players, I didn't want to be the one doing the stacking. The few times I did choose, I always felt downright awful picking my last player.

"Maybe next time," Mr. Martino said to him. "I can split you turkeys up evenly." With his usual good nature, Mr. Martino made our practices and games fun.

"Rosie, you're on the mound first," he said. "I'm the leadoff hitter. Let's see what you got, kid."

I warmed up on three pitches as Mr. Martino stood outside the batting box. Just as he taught us, his eyes followed every pitch as they crossed the plate, and he used his practice swings to embed a perfect stroke in his mind.

"Is that as hard as you can throw?" he jeered. "Is that all the gas you got? Put some mustard on it, Rosie," he continued playfully. "Rock and fire!"

He finally stepped in the box and loosened up his swing and stride. He looked out at Sleepy in center field, and yelled, "This one's coming to you, Sleep!"

I threw an easy fastball and Mr. Martino let it fly by without swinging.

"That's a warning kid," he offered. "I could have blasted that one outta here."

He paused and took two more practice swings before he set himself in the batting box again.

"You've got to mix it up on me," he added.

I took his advice, and threw a change-up that landed low and outside. He swung and blasted a shot down the right field line.

"Foul ball!" he bellowed as if he were the umpire too. "It's your lucky day, pitcher."

"Fan him, Rosie," our first baseman called out.

"He's no hitter," yelled the shortstop.

For the next pitch, I decided to throw the circle change. It was one of Rico's specialties. I made an

OK sign with my right hand and gripped the ball with my middle fingers. I let the ball go and watched it break down and in as it flew over the plate. Mr. Martino's bat foul-tipped it into the backstop.

"He's in trouble now," Sleepy yelled from the outfield. "One more and he's outta there."

Mr. Martino smirked as I took my place on the mound. I pulled the ball and my mitt to my chin, and wound up. I put on the brakes just before I let it go. Mr. Martino's eyes grew wide at the sight of the tantalizing lob. I baited him perfectly. He swung so hard that he spun around. Everyone roared with laughter.

"Took my eye off it," Mr. Martino muttered.

Kids in the field fell over and stomped their feet and mitts against the ground.

"That's exactly what I don't want you kids doing!" Mr. Martino continued. "I just had to show you."

"Yeah, right," Sleepy called out as he laughed hysterically.

After about an hour had passed, I asked someone the score.

"It's seven to two."

"No. It's eight to four."

"What are you talking about? It's seven to three."

"You're cheating!"

Mr. Martino whistled loudly. "Keep arguing and we'll just pack it all up and go home," he said.

Tongues clicked and players rolled their eyes, but that was the end of the dispute. I jogged up to home plate for my turn at bat. Out of the corner of my eye, I saw my dad leaning against the fence. I took a deep breath and focused my eyes on the pitcher. I snapped the bat around, and the ball sailed foul along the first base line.

"You're not getting around quick enough," my father yelled.

Leave me alone! I could feel my face get hot. He was always like a hawk watching every move I made. *Please leave me alone!*

"It's all you, Rosie Jonzie," Mr. Martino yelled to help me relax. "This one's got your name on it."

It wasn't enough to take my father out of my mind. I foul-tipped the next over my head.

"You're dipping the shoulder," he yelled.

He's the coach! I wanted to scream and point at Mr. Martino to make myself clear. But I didn't. Arguing wouldn't have stopped him. My father always yelled out instructions like it was an involuntary reaction. He couldn't help himself. He didn't care where he was either. I used to think that if I were playing in the World Series, he'd have a seat right behind the dugout so he could conveniently throw in his two cents.

I smashed the next ball over the shortstop's head for a single. When my father said nothing, my frustration turned into hurt. *Why didn't he cheer?* He never seemed to realize when I reached this point. It was the point where the only way I could get through without crying was to ignore him. So that's exactly what I did.

Practice ended at eight o'clock sharp. We huddled up on the mound and roared rowdy cheers after Mr. Martino made some rallying cries.

"Let's take it to 'em Saturday!" he hollered. "We're gonna make it look easy! Let's show 'em who we are. This is the big one."

"Who cares?" our grumpy third baseman replied. "We can't make the playoffs. It's impossible."

"So do we just forfeit? Not play? Quit?" Mr. Martino yelled. "No, we're champions! We're fighters! We play 'til the end no matter what! Lemme hear you guys! Winners on three. One... Two... Three... Winners!"

After a few more cheers, we finally broke apart and headed to the parking lot. When my father walked up to Mr. Martino, I stopped in my tracks and started fidgeting. I was sure he was going to say something that would make me look like a player who didn't care about the team.

"How are you doing, Don?" my father asked and he extended his hand. "I just wanted to say thanks for coaching the kids this year."

"Well, it's not over 'til it's over," Mr. Martino said confidently. "And you, young lady, have a whole lot of playing to do this summer."

"Do you know for sure if she's made it?" my father asked anxiously.

"No," he replied just as Sleepy wandered over, "but I've done all I can. They're announcing the all-stars at the concession stand after our game. I won't know for sure until then, just like you. You and Sleepy both deserve to be teammates again. Hang in there, and don't worry about it."

His last words stayed unsettled in my mind. I didn't want Mr. Martino to think that I was so upset that I was losing sleep over all of this. But I knew – and I think Mr. Martino did too – that the thought of my not being on the city all-star team kept my father awake at night.

We said good-bye, and the three of us walked to the car without any more talk of the all-star team. I looked at my best friend, and thought of what it would be like to sit with the fans and watch him play. I quickly dropped the thought from my mind.

"Where's Rico tonight?" my father asked as we drove off. I was still mad at him for yelling at me at practice, so I pretended that I didn't hear him.

"Rosie," he said louder, "where is your brother?"

"I think he's out with Natalie," I muttered, "or his friends. I'm not sure. He made a sandwich for me and said he would see me later."

"He should be working on his swing," my father grumbled, "or working out with the college guys who are home playing in those summer leagues."

"He's doing all that, Dad," I said softly.

"Not as much as he should," he shot back.

I threw in the towel. Somebody had to end it before he really got going. I stared blankly out the window, trying to put my father's words out of my mind. But I couldn't.

It all began when Rico went against my father's advice and jumped right into the minor leagues after passing up a college baseball scholarship. Rico said that he did it because he just didn't like school, and that baseball was everything to him. After a string of nagging injuries, he slipped fast in the world of professional baseball. Without a place to go or an education to help get him a job, he came back home. That's when the problems got even worse.

"I tell ya," my father continued, "he's got his work cut out for him. Working at that garage is going to get old real fast."

He never made the slightest attempt to hide his frustration and disappointment. That's what bothered me more than anything. *Did he ever stop and think of how Rico felt?* It seemed like nothing my brother did would ever please my father again. *If I didn't make the all-star team, would he think I was a failure, too?*

I caught Sleepy watching me in the side mirror. He stuck out his tongue and puffed out his droopy cheeks. I let go of my frown and giggled.

"What's so funny?" my dad asked.

"Nothing," I said laughing as Sleepy kept smiling in the back seat. "You missed it."

"I guess I did," my dad added as we turned down Broadway Ave.

"Rosie struck out Mr. Martino today," Sleepy told my father. "It was so funny. He swung so hard he almost fell over."

"Do you think he did it on purpose or that I really struck him out?" I asked.

"I think he really struck out," Sleepy said. "And then he played it off like he meant to do it on purpose."

"I used the circle change that Rico taught me, for the second strike," I told my father. I always wanted so badly to make him think good things about my brother. "And a super-slow change-up for the third."

"Keep working on your pitching and all your skills so you can play anywhere on the field," he said as he pulled into our driveway. "Both of you."

I quickly glanced up at my father and saw him smile. For one brief second, he seemed proud of me.

Then his smile faded away.

Chapter Three

On Saturday afternoon I swept my raggedy cleats along the tips of the dry center field grass. I looked up and scanned the crowd. My eyes stopped at my father. He was in his usual position, pacing behind the backstop. He kicked a couple of pebbles and then leaned against the chain-link fence.

"What are you blind, Blue?" he called out. "Ahh, come on, Blue...You can do better than that...Maybe all this heat is gettin' to you."

My face burned in embarrassment as I watched the umpire shake his head. All I could do was cross my fingers and hope my father wouldn't push him too far. That's all I needed: my old man thrown out of the ballpark.

I turned to my mother. She was sitting in her favorite purple and green lawn chair with her legs crossed. It was better that she remained seated. Belting out so many cheers nearly wiped her out by the end of every game.

"Be awake out there!" she screamed. "On your toes!"

She looked at me waving and smiling, but I was staring at the empty lawn chair that was propped open next to her. It was for Rico. He was nowhere in sight.

"Wake up, Rosie!" Mr. Martino hollered, snapping me out of my daze. "Only Sleepy can look sleepy."

I quickly understood why Mr. Martino wanted my attention. A big hitter waved his bat angrily above his shoulder as he set himself next to home plate. He took the first pitch, stepped out of the box, and knocked the dirt off his cleats. He stepped back in the box. The pitcher let the ball go, and the batter blasted a shot deep into right field. Our outfielder panicked and charged forward. When the ball sailed clearly over his head, he frantically spun his body around and tripped as he tracked down the ball.

"Get it! Get it!" everyone screamed.

He bent down and his shaking hands fumbled the ball once before he finally got a hold of it. Then he unloaded a poor throw back to our pitcher, who overthrew the third baseman. It was a disaster.

"Let's go!" Mr. Martino shouted to help us out of our shaky inning. "Let me hear you out there!"

Our lead had slipped to a scanty two runs. When the next batter nailed another shot deep into left for a triple, the mood grew serious. Our parents were screaming at us, and my father was leading the way.

"Wake up!" my father screamed impatiently. "Get it together out there! Come on!"

I glared into the opposing team's dugout. Everyone was on his feet. When my eyes turned to the on-deck circle, I took a deep breath. Dennis "Cowboy" Thorpe sauntered his way up to home plate, twirling his bat around in one hand. I looked to my left, and then to my right, and saw both of my teammates backpedaling.

"Ride it outta here, Cowboy," his teammates screamed.

Cowboy was legendary in the league not only because of his power hitting. He was a prankster and a joker — a kid who loved to hot dog every move he made. He squinted and smiled as he pointed his bat out to me in center field. He held his bat in the air for everyone to notice, and his dugout roared. I glared back at him, crouched into my ready position, and eagerly slapped my glove.

"Show-off!" our right fielder called out.

"Come on you chump," grumbled my teammate in left. "I dare you to hit it to her."

A chill ran up my back. I grinned as Cowboy kicked around the dirt until he had both feet set comfortably in the batter's box. To no one's surprise, he took the first pitch. He simply nodded his head as the perfect strike passed him by. Then he calmly stepped out of the box. He looked at our pitcher and tipped his hat in appreciation. The next pitch would be the one with his name on it.

The pitcher delivered the second throw, and Cowboy blasted it up just out of our second baseman's territory. I sprinted in madly from my deep center field position, and shoved my glove out to scoop up the knee-high catch. Just as I caught it, the player on third headed for home. I rifled the ball to Sleepy, who had flipped off his catcher's helmet and stood protecting home plate. Sleepy picked the ball up cleanly after it took one sharp bounce. He swiped his clenched mitt down, and tagged the runner, whose vertical body just touched down in a sprawling slide.

"Yeeerrrr out!" bawled the umpire and we all charged into our dugout.

I looked up and watched my father clap three times. That was it.

"Way to play, Rosie!" Mr. Martino yelled over everyone, including my screaming mother. After we jogged in from the field to the bench, Mr. Martino tapped the bill of my cap. Just as I lifted it back up, I caught a glimpse of Rico walking behind the dugout. When he winked at me and grinned, I knew he had seen my catch. I flipped my hat off and turned it backwards.

"Get us started, Sleep!" Mr. Martino yelled.

Sleepy turned to me just before he jogged up to the plate. "This is gonna be eight," he said with a wide smile.

The number eight had nothing to do with runs. It was all about milkshakes.

"Hammer away, Scotty!" my mother cried out. "Smack it outta here! Keep your eye on it! Do your best! You can do it!"

"Let's go, Sleep!" my dad cheered.

He swung at the second pitch, and nailed a shot into center field. For most kids, it would have been a triple off an error by the outfielder. But not for Sleepy. I could tell by his speed as he rounded third base that my best friend was heading for home, and there was no stopping him.

After the third baseman made the relay catch from the center fielder, he then turned to fire the ball home. Our entire bench rose to its feet just as Sleepy crouched down for his courageous head-first slide into home plate. The throw skimmed the top of the catcher's extended glove and clanged off the backstop. Sleepy smiled as he slapped the plate with the palm of his hand. We ran out of the dugout to celebrate.

"Way to hit the deck," cheered Mr. Martino as he wiped the dirt off Sleepy's belly. My best friend flashed his pearly white grin to the crowd.

"I'll take a vanilla one this time," he yelled to Rico. My brother grinned as he shook his head.

By the end of the inning, we had secured an eight-run lead, and had regained our momentum. I sprinted out to my position in center field. One more inning, and the game was over.

After two easy outs, I waited for our pitcher and the infield to put an end to our spring season. I slapped the smooth leather pocket with the back of my right hand and then turned over my mitt. I looked down at the golden miniature *coquí* charm that I had tied to one of its loose strands. It was a gift my mother had brought back for me from Puerto Rico. She told me how the *coquí* is a lovable singing frog native to her homeland that changes the color of its skin according to its surroundings. It chirps as it hides in the foliage until the sun goes down. She also told me that most people use it as a good luck charm. Standing out in center field all alone, I wondered if luck had anything to do with my making the all-star team.

Our pitcher threw three quick and easy strikes past the last batter for the final out. I pumped my fist in the air and ran into the pitcher's mound to join my teammates. We screamed one last cheer and then headed over to shake the other team's hands. Cowboy stopped in front of me.

"I let you catch that one," he said grinning. "I was just testing you."

I smiled too. Even though I hardly knew him, it seemed tough for anyone to really get mad at a kid like Cowboy.

"That was a nice touch with the double play, Jonzie," he called out to me. I kept smiling.

"Everyone over to the concession stand for the announcement of the all-star team!" Mr. Martino hollered over the commotion. "Both teams."

I took a short breath that stirred butterflies in my stomach. I grabbed my water jug out from under our bench, and walked over to my family with Sleepy at my side. I fidgeted with my *coquí* charm the whole way. I looked up and saw Mrs. Jackson, who hardly had any time to attend our games, chase Sleepy's little brother, Ronnie, as he ran down the third base line.

"Great game!" she said as she ran back out of breath. Sleepy smiled proudly.

"You were fantastic!" my mother added.

"Way to play, kids," my dad said.

Sleepy turned his disarming grin and droopy eyes to Rico.

"The homer doesn't count," Rico said. "It was on too many errors."

"Come on, Rico," Sleepy pleaded. "You never said anything about errors."

"A homer is a homer," I demanded. "He gets the shake."

Rico stood in a stubborn silence scratching his chin. I tugged on his arm and then clung to it. When he lifted me clear off the ground, I clung to him, refusing to let go until he gave in.

"All right, all right," Rico finally admitted as he set me down. "A deal is a deal." Rico reached out, and Sleepy slapped his open palm.

Our group began to stroll over to join the growing crowd at the concession stand. Three coaches stood in a tight semicircle off to the side, glancing down onto a sheet of paper held by Mr. Fonda, the league president. One coach shook his head and stomped away.

"I hope they both make it," Mrs. Jackson mumbled to my mother, who let out a deep sigh as she looked up into the sky.

"Can I have your attention, please," Mr. Fonda raised his voice over the noisy crowd, and I finally looked up. "I'd like to say thank you for coming out and supporting all these kids. Let's give them a round of applause for all their hard work."

Everyone broke into a hearty applause. I looked to the ground and continued to fidget with my *coquí* charm. *What if I don't make it?* Then I looked up at my father. *What would he do if I don't make it? Will he scream and yell, or tell somebody off?*

Rico rested his hand on my shoulder. And finally, Mr. Fonda called out the list. "Lucas Thompkins, Victor DeVito, Dennis Thorpe, Scotty Jackson..."

I looked up at my friend and smiled. He stared at me until all the names had been called.

"... Nick Samanski, Ryan Samanski, and... Rosalinda Jones."

I couldn't believe what I had heard until I felt Rico rubbing his hand on my back.

"Way to go, kid," he said.

Sleepy jumped up and down. I looked up as my dad pressed his lips together in a tight, proud smile. My mom bent down and gave me a kiss.

"Good things do happen, Rosa," she whispered. "You just gotta believe in them, that's all."

I took a deep breath. It was as if a heavy weight had just been lifted off my back. But when I looked up and saw three men pleading with Mr. Fonda, I felt the load all over again. I knew right away it was about me. Mr. Fonda walked straight to his car, ignoring them both.

One man shouted, "She'll be in over her head."

Mr. Fonda's eyes remained fixed on his car. He lowered himself into his car and drove away. I turned away and caught the scowls of two boys as they passed me. My eyes dropped down, and I started to fidget with my charm. I wished that somehow I could fit in with everyone around me. But I couldn't. I was the only girl.

"This is great! This is wonderful!" my mother rambled on. I knew exactly what she was doing. She didn't want me to hear or see what was happening around me. "I'm so proud of you kids."

She looked relieved when Mr. Martino walked over.

"All right, Rosie and Sleepy!" he bellowed. "Way to go, kids!" He gave us each a high five.

"Hey, all-stars!" I heard a loud voice yell.

Sleepy and I turned and saw that it was Cowboy. "If you can't beat 'em, join 'em, right? See you chumps at practice," he said, and he walked away with his back to us. He held his hand over his shoulder and held fingers in a peace sign.

"You even get to play with hot-dog Cowboy, there," Mr. Martino added laughing.

I smiled, knowing how lucky I was to have Mr. Martino around. He almost made me feel as though everything was going to be okay.

But by the sound of things around me, I still had my doubts.

Chapter Four

With my report card clenched in her right hand, my mother stormed through the front door on Monday afternoon. She dropped her keys down, and didn't even bother to say hello.

"You can do much better, Rosa," she said sternly as she waved it at me.

I took it from her hand, opened it up, and scanned down the column of grades. Math: C-, Science: C+, English: C, Social Studies: C-. My shoulders dropped when I exhaled. I dreaded this day for a long time.

"Wait until your father sees it," she warned.

• • • •

I trudged through the front door after basketball practice later that night. My mother stood at the kitchen sink washing dishes, and my father read the paper as he sat at the table eating his dinner. I crossed my fingers and hoped he was in a good mood.

"Hi, honey," he said. "How was practice?"

"Good," I replied.

"Who's coaching?" he asked.

"Mr. O'Malley and Mr. Harris."

"Who's on the team?"

"All of my friends from Broadway," I added with a smile, feeling in complete control of the situation. *Maybe he won't get mad. I'll promise him I'll work harder in the fall.*

"When do you play your games?"

"On Friday nights," I replied.

During our small talk, I felt my mother's dark brown eyes glaring at me. I finally turned to her. When I shrugged innocently, she frowned. Then she moved her eyes to the countertop and then back to me. I followed her stare and saw my report card all by itself. I took a deep sigh and then walked over to pick it up knowing I might as well just get it over with. I moped back to the table and surrendered it to my father. He slipped his glasses on and opened it. As he scanned down the column, his brow furrowed.

"It looks like you took your summer vacation a little too early, Rosalinda," he said firmly.

There was a long pause. So much for his good mood. I began to wring my T-shirt under the kitchen table.

"It's not as if you're not capable or smart enough, that's what gets me," he added, sounding both mad and hurt at the same time. "You shouldn't be just barely getting by."

Then he paused again. This time it was longer. It was the silent treatment. I hated when he did that. I would rather hear him scream and yell from the start than make me sit and agonize over what was going through his mind. I couldn't predict if or when he would blow.

"I think now you should begin making a little better use of your vacation time," he said calmly.

I braced myself for my punishment.

"You're only allowed to watch one baseball game a week."

No big deal. I stood up from my chair and nodded my head in agreement.

"Hold it," he warned. "I'm not through yet. Have a seat."

I sunk down in my chair and bit my bottom lip.

"You have to spend two hours twice a week in the library."

What? I gasped. What about playing with my friends at the park?

My mother spoke up. "And you have to finish at least one 150-page book every two weeks."

I stared at her in disbelief. This is the summer! It is supposed to be my vacation! My mouth dropped open. But nothing came out. They were right about one thing. I was smart enough to know not to scream, cry, or slam any doors. That would have only made matters worse. I walked out of the kitchen and called Sleepy right away.

"Want to go to the library this week?" I mumbled.

"The library?" he answered. "School's over."

"I got in trouble about my grades."

"Oh, no," Sleepy groaned. "Did they yell at you?"

"Not really," I said. "My dad was pretty mad, and my mom agreed with everything he said. I can only watch one baseball game on TV a week and I've got to go to the library twice every week."

"Twice?" he gasped. "It's the summer!"

"Yeah, I know," I grumbled. "And I've got to read a ton of books."

Sleepy moaned.

"You coming?" I asked. There was a pause. "Come on, Sleep."

"Yeah, I guess," Sleepy grumbled.

"I'll call you in the morning."

• • • •

We rode our bikes to the library the next day. Sleepy and I raced down the last block.

"I won," I said.

"No you didn't."

"Fine," I said. "It's a tie."

He settled for the tie as we walked up the steps of the library. I pushed open the door and checked the clock. It was exactly 2:30 in the afternoon.

"We're outta here at 4:30," I whispered to Sleepy.

Sleepy grabbed his stomach as if he was in pain. "I don't know if I can make it," he whined. Then he straightened himself up and broke into a smile.

"Really funny," I groaned.

As we walked deeper into the library, I took a good look around. Books and silence filled the room.

"It smells in here," I said.

Sleepy started sniffing the air. "Yeah," he said, "you're right. It's musty."

"It stinks," I mumbled.

As we slowly drifted around the stacks of books, I started to get tired and bored. I sat down at a table and started to flip through a stack of magazines in the corner. Within a few minutes, I lost interest and began to wander around the stacks again. I tilted my head and read rows of titles, hoping that a 150-page book filled with a lot of pictures and really large print would jump out at me.

"May I help you?" a voice called out.

A gray-haired woman tipped her head down and looked at me from behind her spectacles. I shook my head and shrugged.

"What are you looking for?" she asked politely.

"Nothing," I mumbled.

I shrugged again and looked down. I felt pretty dumb looking for nothing.

"What kinds of things do you like to do?" she persisted.

"Baseball," I answered.

"Easy enough," she said as she turned away. "Follow me."

She led me over to stacks of wooden drawers.

"Do you know what this is called?" she asked.

"The card catalog," I said.

"That's right," she replied.

Of course, I'd been taught how to search the card catalog before. I just didn't feel like doing it.

"We'll start in the children's section," she continued cheerfully, "and if you don't find anything there, or it's too easy for you, we can look through the adult catalog." Her fingers flipped through the index cards and finally stopped at the "Baseball" heading.

"We don't have those fancy computers yet because our library is not that big," she said. "But this does just the same. Jot down the call numbers of the books you might like," she said.

I picked up a pencil off the table and scribbled down the numbers.

"Now follow me," she said.

I hurried to keep up with her. She had a lot of energy for someone cooped up in a library all day.

"See the numbers," she said as she pointed. "You just follow them down, and ... here you go! All the books on baseball you could want."

"Thanks," I muttered.

"I'm Ms. Daniel," she said. "If you need anything let me know."

My eyes were busy scanning the shelves of books. By the time I turned, Ms. Daniel was gone.

For a long time, I stood in the aisle flipping through all kinds of books. I read bits and pieces, hoping to find something just right.

"You find anything yet?" Sleepy whispered as he walked up to me.

I kept my eyes locked on the shelves and said, "I'm still looking."

"Cool," Sleepy said. "Look at all these sports books."

"What'd you get?" I asked.

"I got this one," he held it up. There was a colorful picture of a frightening and gross-looking creature on the front.

"Looks kind of weird," I said.

"Yeah," he added. "It's kind of scary. I've read some like this before."

I chose a book and held it up like a prize. "I'm going to get this one," I said.

"Running the Bases?" Sleepy read the cover. "You're pretty good at that already, Rosie."

"How much time do we have left?" I asked.

Sleepy sprinted to the end of the row of books and peeked up at the clock on the wall. "An hour," he said in a loud whisper.

We goofed off and started giggling as we sat down at the table. I looked up and caught Ms. Daniel's glare and settled down. We read silently until exactly 4:30 p.m. sharp. When the minute hand landed exactly over the six, we both stood up, checked out our books, and said good-bye to Ms. Daniel.

"Will I see you two again?" she asked.

Sleepy looked at me and laughed. I didn't know why. Spending our summer days in the library was not funny.

"Yeah," Sleepy said with a grin. "We'll be back."

Chapter Five

Sleepy and I raced home from the library and dumped our bikes on my front lawn. Just as we reached the front door, the phone rang. I ran in and answered it. It was Tanya, Sleepy's baby-sitter. I handed him the phone.

"I do?" Sleepy shrieked. "Oh, yeah. OK, I'll be right home."

"I almost forgot," Sleepy said to me after he hung up. "I've got a dentist appointment. My mother's coming home to get me. I gotta go."

"I'll see you at practice?"

"Yep," he said with a wide grin as he ran out the door.

I went into my room, got a running start and landed on my bed. Just as I started flipping through my newest box of baseball cards, the front door creaked open. Then I heard the jingle of my mother's keys. She was home from work.

"Let's go, Rosa!" she yelled, and I slipped the top on my box. "Bring your book."

I hopped off my bed with my tattered mitt in one hand and my shiny book in the other. I skipped into the living room and smiled as my mother's eyes fell upon me.

"Let me see what you picked out," she asked. I proudly held my book up for her to see.

"Baseball, baseball, baseball," she sighed. "What are we going to do with you?"

I shrugged and grinned. We hurried into the car and drove off to meet Rico. Ten minutes later, she stopped in front of the garage. The rhythmic thumping of merengue music blared from the open door. I watched Rico strut out of the garage as he twisted his hands in an oily rag. He rested his forearm on the window, leaned down, and winked at me.

"Where's practice?" he asked.

"Tucker Park at 6:30," my mother replied. "Make sure she reads while she's waiting."

I rolled my eyes.

"You have half-an-hour before practice, Rosa," she added.

I nodded and she kissed me on the cheek. "I'll see you tonight," she said. "Have fun at practice."

I didn't say good-bye. I was still bothered that my mother was in on this reading thing, too. She knew how hard my father was on me, and most of the time she stuck up for me. On a few occasions, she argued with him so much about the way he treated me and Rico that she wouldn't talk to him for days. This time I really wanted her to feel sorry for me about my reading punishment. But she didn't. My mother never took any excuses for getting poor grades in school.

After I slammed the car door, I stepped alongside my brother and he rested his wrist on my shoulder.

"Let me see your book," he said.

I showed it to him, and he chuckled. "What did Mama say when she saw it?" he asked.

"She just shook her head," I said plainly.

"Well, at least you're reading," he said seriously and then he paused. "You don't realize how important it is right now."

"But it's the summer," I said.

"Doesn't matter," he replied.

Rico was no longer smiling. Hearing me talk about not wanting to read and not caring about school brought his mind back to his own troublesome past.

"It's just like baseball, kid," he said softly. "When do you think the pros work their hardest?"

I shrugged as Rico frowned.

"Everybody has to practice during the season," he began, "just like everyone has to go to school. But not everybody is out there during the off-season, and that's what makes the difference." He paused and finally let out what he was trying to say all along. "You don't want to end up like me — wishing you had done things differently."

It took a lot for my brother to admit what he had just said. At the age of 22, Rico had finally retired what my parents called an "invincibility complex." I used to hear them argue about it all the time. It wasn't that my brother was a bad person. It was just that he had a hot temper occasionally, and he hung out with what my parents called "the wrong crowd." When Rico and his friends got together, they acted like nothing or nobody could stop them no matter what. Most of them ended up in jail at an early age. And as far as school, he and most of his friends never took it seriously. With his mind filled only with playing professional baseball, he barely made it through high school.

"You can stay in the office," he said as we walked through the dark garage. Along with the rhythmic beat of the music, a thick smell of gasoline and oil filled the air. A man in a blue worksuit had his head under the hood of a car. When he slowly lifted his head up, he turned our way and grinned. It was Eduardo, who was one of my brother's oldest friends.

"Hey, it's the girl who's going to make it in the big leagues!" he yelled over the music. "Rico told me you made the all-star team. You're going to be famous, Little Jonzie. I'm going to see that long pony tail of yours on television and be cheering for you. I'll be telling everyone that I knew you when you were a baby."

I shrugged my shoulders in embarrassment.

"Don't forget me," Eduardo joked. He smiled before he stuck his head back under the hood.

I followed Rico into the back office, and sat down on an old, torn car seat in the corner. After being at the library all afternoon, everything in the garage seemed so loud. When he shut the door behind him, the music, screeching and rattling noises faded. Rico reached into an unbalanced refrigerator and pulled out a bottle of iced tea.

"Thanks," I said as he handed it to me.

I glanced around the office. Above the mess of papers and keys on the desk was a framed picture of Roberto Clemente. Rico also had a poster of him in his room.

"You should find a book on Roberto," he suggested.

I nodded my head. Deep inside, I really wanted to ask Rico something that I never had the courage to ask. *Why don't you read? Why don't you go back to school?*

But I didn't say anything. Whenever my father brought up Rico's past or even mentioned school, Rico flew off the handle. He had settled down in the last few months, but he still had a lot bottled up inside of him. No matter how much my father wanted to help, Rico always told him that he would never understand. Ever since junior high, my brother considered himself closer to my mother's Puerto Rican roots. Rico always claimed my father couldn't understand him because he was white. When Rico said these things, my father's hurt quickly turned into anger. I usually ran into my room, stuck my head under my pillow, and begged for all of the shouting to stop.

It's a hard thing to explain, and even more difficult to understand. Before I was born, I heard my mother and father had to constantly answer to family members who did not feel people of two different backgrounds should get married. My mother told me that it was very tough to deal with people for a long time. But she said that by the time I was born, people on both sides of the family had begun to think differently. As much as everything seemed to be OK, I still wondered about where I fit in.

One day after another argument between my brother and father, I thought about choosing an identity. I asked my mother if I had to. She told me that I most certainly did not.

"You have brought so many people back together," she said. "Just be yourself and others will see how foolish it is for them to be seeking differences."

Then I thought of all my friends on Broadway Ave. Molly, Wil, Angel, and I were all a little different from each other and we all got along just fine. I decided that I would remain as I was. Just like everyone else, I was part of my mother and a part of my father.

I put my eyes on the pages of my book and started to read. My mind quickly drifted into the history of the game and the best players of all-time. I read about players like Crafty Max Carey, who studied how to be a better base stealer. And then there was my favorite —James Cool Papa Bell. One person said that Papa Bell was so fast that he could turn out the light and jump in bed before the room got dark. I laughed out loud, thinking of how great it would be to be able to move that fast, or to have people call me Rosie Cool Mama Jones.

• • • •

An hour later, Rico opened the door, startling me.

"How's the book?" he asked.

"Good," I said. "I like it."

We said good-bye to Eduardo as we stepped into the Mustang. When Rico pulled into the parking lot, I looked out onto the field and saw three boys already warming up.

"Dad's picking you up," Rico told me. "I'm going to stay for a while. My game isn't until seven."

"You don't have to stay," I told him. "Sleepy will be here with me."

As much as I loved having Rico around, I didn't want my coaches or new teammates to think that I was scared to face a new team on my own.

"All right," he conceded. "There's Sleepy now."

Sleepy jumped out of his mother's car, and Rico hit his horn and waved. He looked over at me and patted me on the knee. "Go get 'em kid," he said and I popped out of the car.

"How was the dentist, Sleep?" I asked as we met.

"No cavities," he said proudly, and I smiled.

As we walked onto the field, a stocky man with jeans and a green baseball cap approached us.

"Hi, kids," he said. "I'm Coach Samanski. Go ahead and warm up with the rest of the guys until everyone gets here."

Sleepy and I tossed the ball back and forth. I looked to my side and caught a quick glimpse of the Samanski twins warming up.

"Nice throw," one said to the other sarcastically as he chased down a poor toss by his brother.

"Well, maybe if you could catch," the other shot back.

I made eye contact, and then shifted my eyes away. I looked past Sleepy to see Cowboy hop off his bike and gently lean it against the backstop. He strolled on over to the field and extended his hand to our coach.

"Nice to meet ya, sir," Cowboy said in a phony southern drawl. "The name is Dennis. But you can call me Cowboy."

"All right, Cowboy," he said. "I'm Coach Samanski."

"Do you mind if I call you Coach Ski?" Cowboy asked. "It sounds cool."

"That's fine with me," he replied.

Cowboy smiled as he scooped up a ball and heaved it straight up in the air above his head. He reached up and plucked it out of the air.

Wil had told me that Dennis "Cowboy" Thorpe had earned his nickname one Halloween when he dressed up as a man straight from the saloons of the Wild West. He wore a stiff cowboy hat, an oversized blue vest, and matching cowboy boots. He liked the boots so much that he wore them almost every day to school that year – so much that the kids started calling him Cowboy.

"Bring it in," Coach Samanski yelled. Some of us jogged, others walked fast.

"Hustle in, guys," he hollered again.

"And girls," someone quipped.

I didn't flinch. It wasn't like I'd never heard that one before.

We all crowded around home plate. Coach Samanski introduced himself again.

"We can call him Coach Ski," Cowboy interrupted, and he looked back at our coach. "Oh, sorry."

Coach Ski then introduced his assistant, Dr. Meyers.

"You can call me, Doc," said the gray-haired man with an easy smile and a round belly.

"Why don't you go around and introduce yourselves?" Coach Ski asked. "Be sure to tell us your nicknames. Let's start with you, Scotty."

"I'm Scotty Jackson," my best friend said with a smile. "But everybody calls me Sleepy."

Next to him sat a thin-framed boy with jet-black hair, milky skin, and periwinkle eyes. "I'm John Meyers," the boy said. "Everybody calls me Fishbone or just Fish."

We went around the circle from Nick and Ryan Samanski to Victor and Luke. When it was Cowboy's turn, he simply said, "I'm Cowboy. Just Cowboy."

The team burst out laughing at Cowboy. Then he broke into a smile himself.

Just as the laughter subsided, I said softly, "I'm Rosie Jones."

"Speak up, young lady!" Coach Ski shot back.

My face burned in embarrassment. "I'm Rosie," I repeated.

"I didn't hear you," he said again.

The weight of everyone's stare fell upon me. I glared at my coach and refused to repeat myself again.

"If you plan on being heard, you've got to speak up," Coach Ski said firmly. Then he moved on to the next person beside me.

I shot him a dirty look that he didn't see. He didn't have to say I wasn't loud enough. He didn't have to call me a young lady. Everybody knew I was a girl. And I would have been willing to bet that everyone in the league knew my name for that very same reason.

When we finished our introductions, Coach Ski called us up on our feet to stretch. "Cowboy you lead and then everyone take two laps around the field."

We spread out and then formed four straight lines along the left side of the diamond. Cowboy stood proudly in front of our stretching lines and took command.

"All right, City Sluggers!" he called out our team name. "Let's stretch out those muscles. We all know we're not getting any younger."

Doc Meyers smiled, but Coach Ski frowned. "Let's go, Cowboy," he said.

Cowboy called out the counts as if he were a military sergeant. He even had us clapping when we reached ten.

"Hey, Sleepy," Cowboy hollered. "No snoozing on me!"

"I can't hear you, Fish!" he yelled at Fishbone. "Let me hear ya, partner."

Fish piped up as did the rest of the group. I looked over at Scotty and we both giggled at how much fun Cowboy was. I looked around, and everyone was smiling. Except the twins. They looked so serious, like they were stuck in a bad mood. I looked hard at them, trying to find some way to distinguish between the two. I couldn't see any differences.

"How do we tell you apart?" Fish finally asked one of them.

"That's Nick," Ryan said firmly. "He wears a batting glove all the time. I never wear one. After a while, you'll be able to tell us apart. It's easy."

"Hey!" Coach Ski snapped. "Enough chatting. We've got a lot work to do."

He looked right at me when he yelled. I looked away in disgust. *How could I be the one talking when he just screamed at me for not being loud enough?* I knew right then that I was in for a long night.

We fired line drives and some grounders at each other to test our agility and hand-eye coordination. Half of us then split up to throw around the heavy ball as the others practiced receiving hits in the field and making the throw to first base.

"Second group, come on over!" Coach Ski hollered. We shuffled over to the infield as the other group passed us. Cowboy knocked Sleepy's hat down below his eyes, and then laughed as Sleepy tried to chase him down.

Cowboy turned to me and asked, "Hey, Rosie, do you talk?" I looked at him and didn't say a word. He grinned. "I'll have you talking soon enough. You'll be causing all kinds of problems."

"Let's go!" Coach Ski yelled from home plate. "No more horsing around, Cowboy. Sleepy take third, Vic take short, Fish on second, and Nick at first."

I stood behind Sleepy and Vic at third and short, and Luke backed up Nick at second. Coach Ski cracked hits to the infield, and rotated them around so each player had a shot at playing every position. Luke and I just watched. After about five minutes, I looked over at Luke for an explanation. He shrugged his shoulders.

"Luke take Vic's spot," Coach Ski yelled. He said nothing to me, and just kept hitting. I stood up straight and folded my arms across my chest, knowing I had already been forgotten – or ignored.

Five minutes later, Doc whispered something to Coach Ski. Coach Ski grudgingly stopped and turned his attention to the infield.

"Rosie, take John's spot at short," he hollered.

My heart skipped a beat, and I hustled over to take Fishbone's position. Coach Ski hit the ball around the infield again. The first hit to me was a soft dribbler. The second was an easy pop fly. The third was a line drive right at me.

"Bring it in," he yelled to both groups, and he waved us in his direction.

What? I glared at my short, pudgy coach. *How can I show you anything on three lousy hits?*

As I jogged in with my teammates, Coach Ski called out, "Nice job, guys."

Then he split us up for batting practice. Each person got up to bat five times before we rotated around the field and in to hit. Coach Ski was the pitcher. Sleepy got up and cracked three out of his five pitches. Cowboy followed him, and nailed four nice ones. When he whiffed completely on his fifth, he said, "Didn't want you to lose your confidence, Coach."

Nick stepped up to bat with a serious scowl. His father increased the speed of his pitches, and Nick swung hard. He hit the ball to shortstop.

"Come on, Nick," Coach Ski scolded him. "Get it out of the infield."

Nick's face turned red and he gritted his teeth. On the next two pitches, he slapped clean shots to the outfield.

"That's a little better," Coach Ski said. Nick dropped his bat down off his shoulder, and walked back to the bench frowning. Ryan stepped up to the plate, and crushed all five balls deep in the outfield. He smiled on every one.

I was up next. I hurried in to strap on my batting glove, and rushed up to the plate. He lobbed the first pitch and I sent it over the second baseman's head. He lofted another one. I grounded it to short. *Come on!* I needed some heat. When the third pitch was lobbed, I was furious. *What is going on?*

But I knew the answer to that already. I just didn't want to believe that my own coach wouldn't even give me a chance. I wasn't a real player in his mind. I looked at his fat belly and stumpy legs and thought rotten things about him. Then I drilled my last pitch right back at him. He flinched, but managed to catch it anyway. Then he yelled, "Next batter up!"

"Good job, Rosie," Doc said to me as I set my bat in the dugout. The sympathetic look in his brown eyes wasn't enough to make my anger and humiliation go away.

"You got it, Rosie," he added softly. I refused to look at him. As far as I could see, Doc was no better than Coach Ski. If he was, he would have said something. But he didn't. I wondered if we were all playing for the same team or if I was out there all by myself.

My father pulled up in his car just as practice ended. He opened the door and slammed it shut. As he approached the field, I crossed my fingers and hoped that he wouldn't say anything. I just wanted to go home.

"Let's hit a couple," Sleepy said as he saw my dad beginning to chat with the coaches. Nick was pitching to Ryan. Luke and Victor were out in the field. I ran into the dugout to get one last gulp of water.

"Hurry up," Sleepy yelled.

I jogged out and bent over to pick up my glove off the grass. Just as I stood up, I saw this black blur flying at my face. Then I felt a hard, crushing blow to my head. Ryan's foul ball had jumped off his bat, ricocheted off the ground and caught me square in the right eye. I felt the bump of swelling grow larger by the second. I covered it up with my glove, and bent over to the ground. I clenched my teeth together and refused to cry. I couldn't. Not in front of my new team. Not in front of Coach Ski.

"Are you okay, honey?" I heard my dad say. I took my glove off my face and opened my eyes. I nodded my head.

"You got a nice one," my dad added as he held me closer to him. "You're lucky you didn't get knocked out cold."

Coach Ski handed my father a cold pack. "You gotta be careful, Rosie" Coach Ski said. "You've always got to be aware of what's going on."

My father took one long look at him and shook his head as he punched the plastic pack. He gently pressed it against my eye and held it there as we walked to the car. I didn't want to look like a wimp, so I reached up to hold the ice pack myself.

"I got it, Dad," I said and I pushed his hand away.

"All right, fine," he said. "I was just trying to help."

"She should probably take it easy," Coach Ski yelled out to us.

"She'll be fine," my dad called out in a frustrated tone. "She'll be back on Thursday." It sounded like my father was getting the same bad feeling I was from Coach Ski.

"You sure you're okay, Rosie?" Sleepy asked as we got in the car. "He hit you pretty hard. I saw it."

"I'm fine," I mumbled.

Later that night, I rested my head on my mother's shoulder as we sat in the living room watching television. I watched her as she struggled to hold her head up. Only a few seconds passed before her neck muscles gave in and her chin dropped to her chest. Then her eyes popped open and she lifted her head up again.

"Ma," I whispered, "I don't think I can read my books this week or go to the library."

"Really?" she replied with her eyes closed. "That means you won't be able to go to practice if your sight is that bad."

My mother opened her eyes and grinned. She wasn't as dazed and confused as I had hoped. I smiled too, but it soon faded and I looked away. I thought about all the things Coach Ski said to me that night at practice. He made me feel like dirt.

An hour later, I felt a hand gently lift my chin up. I opened my eyes. It was Rico.

"Shhh," he said quietly. "Take it easy, kid. You got a nice one there. You okay?"

"Uh-huh," I answered groggily.

"Did you win?" I asked.

"Yep," he said.

"Did you hit a homer for me?" I asked.

"Yep," he said.

I smiled a funny-looking one-eyed smile, and Rico grinned. His soft brown eyes, which looked like they had been there and seen it all, told me not to worry. I hugged my brother, and held all of my tears inside me. He picked me up and carried me to my bedroom. After he left, I finally began to cry. I hated to cry. I wasn't crying because of my eye. That was nothing compared to what really hurt.

No one would ever understand why I didn't want to go back to practice.

Chapter Six

When I walked onto the courts at the Anderson Park the next day, everybody turned and stared. Molly stopped dribbling and winced. She tucked her basketball under her arm, and walked closer to me.

"What the heck happened, Rosie?" she asked.

"I got hit with a ball at practice last night," I mumbled as my friends huddled around.

"That's gonna turn all kinds of colors," Wil said.

"It must have hurt," Angel added.

I flipped my hat forward with the bill in the front and pulled it down low.

"Don't flip your cap," Penny said. "Show it off. You're looking tough."

I dropped my head in shame. There I was, thinking of quitting baseball, and my friends were calling me tough.

"How was practice?" Angel asked.

"Okay," I said.

"Just okay?" Penny asked curiously. I kept my eyes fixed in the distance. "What's going on, Rosie?"

"Nothing," I mumbled.

"Shoot 'em up!" interrupted J.J. as he walked down from the other end of the court. I took a deep breath as my friends all turned away from me. J.J.

had saved me from any further questioning about my baseball troubles.

The usual Broadway crowd flooded the courts and lined up on the free-throw line for one shot each. The first five players who made it played against the second set of five. Billy, Wil, Penny, Molly, and I made our shots, which left Eddie, Angel, Marvin, Sleepy, and J.J. on the other team.

"You're always with Penny," J.J. yelled at Molly. "That's not fair."

Molly grinned devilishly at J.J. and said, "I made the shot."

Everybody wanted to be on Penny's team. She could play any position in virtually every sport, and she even got straight A's in school. She never seemed to have a worry or fear about anything. Kids in the neighborhood not only wanted to hang out with her, they wanted to be Penny Harris.

"We're switching teams after this game," J.J. muttered.

"No we're not," said Eddie, who was the biggest bully on Broadway. "We're gonna win."

As the bragging and arguing went back and forth, Penny kept smiling. After neatly tucking in her shirt, she adjusted her navy blue headband. Then her eyes shifted around to check if everyone was ready to go. She clapped twice, put her hands up, and the ball sailed in her direction. Her eyes narrowed as she called out, "Ball is in!"

When the game began, I ran around doing my best to stay in the mix of things. I picked up a steal, then dished a bounce pass to Penny. I took a horrible shot, but Penny got the rebound. I passed another one to Molly. She banked her shot off the backboard, and it went into the basket.

"Nice pass, Rosie," she said.

I jumped after another loose ball, and Eddie tackled me.

"What are you playing?" Molly screamed at Eddie. "Football?"

"I didn't mean it," Eddie shouted back.

I dragged myself up off the ground. The thought of retaliating never entered my mind. Even if I had a running start, I don't think I could have moved Eddie's solid frame. I let his foul go, and just hoped he wouldn't "accidentally" do it again. On the next play, Angel scratched me with one of her long fingernails. I clicked my tongue as I grabbed my bleeding hand.

"Sorry," she said as she shrugged innocently.

"Would you cut those things!" Wil snapped at Angel.

I jumped back into the action, only to have Marvin push me on the next play. I scowled at him. When Eddie shoved me again, I decided that was enough. I glared up at him. I was sick and tired of being bumped, shoved, and scratched. So I fought back the best way I knew how. I picked the ball out of Eddie's reach on the next play. Then I double-teamed J.J. in the corner. I was everywhere, defending everyone. On offense, Eddie tried to steal the next ball from me. This time I protected myself. He accidentally caught one of my elbows in his chest.

"Ow!" he yelped as I zipped past him and scored a lay up. Two plays later, I stole the ball from Angel.

"Way to play, Rosie!" Penny cheered as she gave me five.

We played basketball until late in the afternoon, and somehow we managed to make it through without one argument, any tears shed, or anyone mumbling, "I quit."

"Now only if we could be quiet and play like that everyday," said Penny, shaking her head.

In a neighborhood like ours, where emotions ran wild, it took a very strong person not to raise a voice or hand. Molly stood up for everyone and everything, which landed her in a fair share of fights. Wil could argue something forever, and she was always very skilled at talking her way out of physical confrontations. Although I wasn't a fighter like Molly, I did become involved in group shoving matches, and took pride in being an ace at getting under people's skin. I tried not to fight because if my mother heard I was swinging at anything besides a baseball, she would have dragged me home by the ear. As for Penny and Angel, they almost always kept their cool or just laughed things off.

"Come on, Wil!" Molly yelled. "Hurry up!"

Wil remained hunched over the running water fountain.

"Some time this week," Molly nagged.

"Time is up," Penny quipped.

Wil lifted her head up and wiped her chin with the back of her hand. "It's too hot to argue," she said. Then she purposely stepped on Penny's toes, and covered her mouth.

"OOPS," said Wil giggling.

"Ha, ha," said Penny. She let it go.

"Who needs a ride to practice tonight?" Molly asked.

"I do," I said. "My dad's gonna pick me up, though," I added. "We can give somebody a ride home if you want."

"You can come with us," Penny assured me.

• • • •

Later that evening, I walked down to the Harris's and waited on the porch for Penny to come outside.

"No fighting at practice," Penny joked as she skipped down her stairs and onto the sidewalk. Her little brother, Little Sammy, burst through the aluminum door. He caught a glimpse of my purple eye and winced.

"What happened?" he gasped.

"She got hit with a baseball at practice," Penny explained.

I thought about telling Penny about my rotten coach. Then I quickly changed my mind. I never complained. If I did, she would think I wasn't as tough as everybody thought. Penny wouldn't understand. She didn't have any worries. She was so good at everything.

Mr. Harris followed Sammy out the door. "Is that baseball team treating you all right?" he asked.

"Yeah," I mumbled.

"By the looks of things, you must have had one rough first practice."

"I just got hit that's all," I said quietly.

"Hang in there," Mr. Harris told me, "and you'll get what's coming to you." I looked up at Penny, and she nodded her head in assurance.

Why does everyone keep telling me that? What if things don't work out?

Once we arrived at the gym, I let my baseball troubles go and focused on basketball. I ran out onto the court with my friends and lined up for our shooting games. I knocked Molly out of two games by making my shot before she did.

Losing was always a difficult thing for Molly, and being beaten by a baseball player made it all the more painful. But Molly O'Malley would never give up. In the middle of the third game, she pushed my ball into the corner of the gym.

"Cheater!" Wil screamed to my defense.

Even though I said nothing, I was determined to get Molly back. I ran back into the game and quickly sunk my shot, which knocked Molly out again. With her lips pursed, she slammed the ball down.

"We're playing again!" she called out in frustration.

Before I could respond, the whistle shrieked and our small rivalry became a thing of the past. We formed our lay-up lines, played our shooting games, and ran through our offense. With about a half-hour left in practice, I saw something red out of the corner of my eye. My father was wearing his favorite red nylon sweatsuit – the same suit he wore practically every night after work. Rico and I joked that we could see him coming from miles away. My father sat down on the bleachers by the door, and folded his arms in front of him.

Mike, J.J., Eddie, Marvin, and Beef Potato strolled in the gym for our open scrimmage time.

"I'm feeling it tonight," J.J. said. "You better look out."

"What, are you going to make two baskets tonight instead of just one?" Penny joked and we all laughed.

"I'm just warning you now," J.J. added with a smile.

All of the boys lived on Broadway, except for Beef. None of us knew Beef's real name. All we knew is that his brother named him Beef for his hearty appetite, and then somebody else gave him Potato as a last name. It was fun to call him Beef, and he always answered to it with no offense taken.

"What's up, Beef?" Penny said.

"Nothin' much," he replied. "Man, it's hot in here."

After he wiped his brow, he reached up and ripped down a rebound.

"Hi, guys," Mr. O'Malley said. "Lace 'em up, and hustle on out."

J.J. threw his hands up in the air when he looked at me. "No fighting today," he said.

I forced a weak smile.

"You should have seen what she did to the other guy," Beef joked.

Everybody laughed, except for me. I didn't like all the attention being drawn to me.

"Let's get started," Mr. Harris said to settle everyone down.

Mr. O'Malley tossed the ball up for the start of the scrimmage. I sprinted down each end of the floor, and tried to stay as involved as possible. It was tough to run around with one eye swollen half-shut, while trying to keep up with the best player in the city. Penny dribbled, passed, and shot the ball effortlessly. I always had this special feeling as I was running down the floor with her on my team. No matter how many points she could score, Penny always passed the ball and cheered for everyone. She made us all feel important.

In the opening minutes of practice, Penny threw me an incredible pass, but I missed the lay up.

"Sorry," I mumbled as we ran down the floor.

"Shake it off," Penny said. "You'll get it next time."

"Come on, Rosie!" my dad hollered. "Put it in the basket."

I clenched my fist and pumped my arms as I ran down the floor. *Please just for once — leave me alone!* But that was asking too much. My father was an insurance salesman who claimed to be an expert in everything, including basketball.

I stole the ball back, and passed it to Wil for a shot under the basket. She swished it.

"Way to play, Rosie!" Mr. O'Malley yelled.

Not one cheer came from my father. Of course when I missed two easy shots, he had something to say. "Get your head in the game," he screamed. "Make a shot! You're not concentrating!"

How can I concentrate when a screaming lunatic, who also happens to be my father, is all over my back?

"You got to work on those lay ups, Rosa," were the first words out of his mouth when I walked over at the end of practice. "You've got to use your body better under the basket."

What body? I looked down at my string-bean body, and tried to imagine what I looked like when I drove underneath the basket to the area where Beef Potato roamed.

"Hi, girls," my dad said to my friends and he smiled. "When are we playing one-on-one, Penny?" he asked.

Penny smiled sheepishly. He turned back towards me, and rested his hand gently on my head. "Your mother has dinner waiting for us."

No one needed a ride, so we drove home together. My father talked about the top professional baseball players. I just sat there barely listening.

"Did you go to the library today?" he asked.

"No," I said. "I went yesterday."

"Oh," he said. "How's that working out? Your mother tells me that you've been reading a baseball book."

"Yeah," I said and I looked back out the window again.

Then finally, my father asked about what was really on his mind. "You like the all-star team, Rosa? They look like a good team."

"It's OK," I said. "That kid Cowboy is funny."

"Coach Samanski said he's going to try and give everyone equal playing time this weekend," my dad told me. "He said that it's really important for the city to finish first in the state this year. They lost in the championship last year. I just told him that you'd play any position he needed."

I listened quietly to my father trying to figure it all out. Sometimes I really enjoyed being around him. He was smart, and sometimes he was really funny. He made my friends laugh and took us out for ice cream. But when I played sports, it was like he turned into a different person. I never knew if he was really proud of me. I wondered whether he really cared about my happiness or if he just cared about his own.

When we got home that night, I walked into the kitchen and greeted my mother. "Where's Rico?" I asked.

"He's over at Natalie's," my mother said. "He said he'd be home to eat."

I sighed. Between his working at the garage, playing ball, and spending too much time with what's-her-name, we had a hard time catching up with one another.

"What's wrong?" my mother asked.

"Why does he always have to be over with her?" I grumpily demanded.

"They care about each other," she said simply.

I still didn't understand what all the fuss was about. It was just some girl. When I heard the front door open, I eagerly stuck my head out into the living room. My smile disappeared when I saw Natalie step into our house. She wore a ridiculous red bow in her hair that would have gone great with my dad's loud sweat suit.

"Hi, Rosie," Natalie said as Rico gently closed the door behind him.

I mumbled a hello and turned back to the table. So much for talking to my brother that night.

My dad dropped his newspaper down from in front of his face.

"Hi," Rico said.

"Did you have a game tonight?" my father asked.

"No," my brother replied. "I've got one tomorrow."

"Have you heard from your agent recently?" my father asked.

"No," Rico replied. "I'm going to call him early next week."

"Are you still working out with those college guys? I'm telling you – that's what you need to be doing."

"I am," Rico muttered in embarrassment. "Tomorrow we're working out."

My eyes grew wide and I held my breath. I didn't want this to explode into another shouting match.

"Yeah, tomorrow," my father said as he pulled the newspaper back up in front of his face. "Tomorrow is too late."

My heart ached as I watched Rico's eyes drop to the ground. He grabbed Natalie's hand.

"We're going to go out to eat," he said firmly. "Good night." He slammed the door behind him.

I took a deep breath as my mother emerged from the kitchen. Her eyes narrowed as she glared at my father. "Why do you have to be so hard on him?" she pleaded. "You will drive him away for good if you keep it up."

"Somebody needs to be on him," my father said harshly.

"He's working hard," my mother shot back.

"Why are you always defending him?"

"Somebody has to," she answered.

"Every day that passes makes it only harder for him to make it," my father said. "He might be too late already."

My mother shook her head and walked back into the kitchen. She picked up a washcloth and stuck her hands into the sink. Loose strands from her bun of hair hung down over her brown almond eyes. She started to hum a song.

I walked over to my mother, picked up the towel and began to dry the dishes.

"Mama," I asked. "Do you think Rico's ever gonna make it in baseball?"

My mother's hands stopped. She blew the hair out of her face and looked down at me.

"I believe Rico will make it," she said. "I just don't know how much it really matters in the end if playing baseball is that important. I just want him to be happy with his life — whatever he chooses to do. If he is happy, that will always be good enough for me."

My mother spoke from her heart, and I believed her. But she didn't give me the answers I needed to hear.

What will make Rico happy?

Chapter Seven

A roll of thunder shook the sky, and stirred me from my sleep the next morning. I heard a steady shower of rain pounding the ground outside. I pulled my sheet over my head. I hated rain. Nobody went to the park in a thunderstorm. Some of us tried, but within minutes, parents were on their porches or opening windows and screaming at us to get inside.

There was one good thing about the rain that day. If it lasted until the evening, baseball practice would be canceled. No baseball, no Coach Ski. I sat up from my bed and stared out the window with a new appreciation for Mother Nature.

A syrupy aroma pulled me up from my bed and into the kitchen. I sat down at the kitchen table and dug into pancakes topped with slices of mangos and bananas.

"Can Sleepy come over today?" I asked.

"I don't know," my mother said. "I've got some errands to run. Why don't you use this day to go to the library? I'll drop you off and pick you up."

I huffed and sighed. It seemed like I practically lived at the library.

"Well?" she asked.

"Okay," I mumbled.

After breakfast I called Sleepy, and he agreed to go with me. Five minutes later, he was at our door. We sprinted through the rain to our car in the driveway, covering up our books by tucking them under our T-shirts.

"It's locked," my mother yelled from the porch. "You kids have all the energy in the world," she added as she hustled out underneath her umbrella. "Now if you only put it to use in school."

When she dropped us off, I reminded her to come exactly two hours later.

"Promise?" I asked.

"I'll do my best," she assured me. "I know spending an extra five minutes there could make you terribly sick."

It very well could have. She didn't know how bad those musty books smelled, and that awful, annoying silence could drive a person crazy.

Sleepy and I walked through the library doors, and Ms. Daniel greeted us with a big smile.

"It's good to see you two again," she said breaking the deafening silence. "What are your names?"

"I'm Sleepy and this is Rosie," he said.

"I just love to see kids here in the summer," she added proudly.

I glanced at Sleepy, who knew exactly what I was going through my mind. *If she only knew the truth.*

"What are you two looking for today?" Ms. Daniel asked.

"I'm going to finish my book," Sleepy said.

"Me too," I added.

We both sat down at a table. I looked around in the empty library. "This stinks," I whispered.

"What?" Sleepy said as he picked his head up from reading his book.

"That I have to be here," I mumbled.

"Well, you're not here by yourself," Sleepy reminded me.

He was right. I couldn't look back into his droopy eyes without smiling. I picked up a piece of paper, crumpled it up and threw it at him. We started giggling as we threw balled up pieces of paper at each other.

"Shhhh!" Ms. Daniel hushed. "You throw things on the field but not in here!" she scolded.

I glanced at her and then stared down at the table. I opened my book and started to read. After I turned the last page, I eagerly looked up at the clock. Then I took a deep breath. Time wasn't passing fast enough. I still had over an hour left. I sat in my seat for a few minutes doing nothing at all. The silence almost put me to sleep. I really didn't want to get another book, so I just continued to stare around the room in a daze. Then Sleepy's elbow jabbed in my side.

"You done?" he said.

I nodded.

"So am I," he said. "Let's get another one."

What? I was stunned by his enthusiasm for learning, especially in the summer.

"You should try reading one of the scary ones," he said excitedly.

There was no way I could argue with him because he had already made a run for the stacks. I pulled myself out of my wooden seat and followed my best friend.

"Once you read one, you just want to read them all," he said.

Sleepy gave it his best, but he couldn't sell me on his favorites. I returned to the sports section and picked up another baseball book. It was about the same length as my last book. When I sat down and began reading again, time flew by. I looked up at the clock, and was happy to see that our stay was officially over. We checked out our new books, said good-bye to Ms. Daniel, and then waited just outside the door under the awning to keep us from getting wet until my mom arrived.

"How was your day?" my mother asked.

"Fine," I said. "Maybe I should just work there," I said sarcastically. "I spend enough time in that place."

"That's a great idea," my mother said. "I'll bring it up to your father tonight at dinner. I think he would like that idea."

I groaned. My mother turned and raised her eyebrows at me. "You better watch what you say, Rosalinda. Remember that you brought this upon yourself."

I didn't totally bring it upon myself. Rico helped. If he hadn't slacked off in school as much as he did, I wouldn't be confined to a library twice a week. He never had to do this. Now I had to face twice as much punishment. It wasn't fair.

"Looks like it's clearing up," Sleepy said as we drove down Broadway Ave. I looked out the window and watched as slanted streaks of rain continued to fall from the sky.

"I don't think so, Sleep," I said.

Just before dinner, the phone rang, and I jumped to it. It was Coach Ski. "Rosie, the fields are a mess," he said. "There's no practice. We've got a double header this weekend at Friar Park on the East Side.

First game starts at 2:00. Be there at 1:30. Are your parents coming?"

"Yeah," I said.

"Will you tell Sleepy?"

"Uh-huh," I said.

"Good. See you Saturday."

I hung up the phone and broke the news to Sleepy. "No practice," I said, shrugging my shoulders.

"It's not that bad," Sleepy said wistfully as he jumped up to look out the window again. He then turned to me as I sat on our couch glued to the television.

"What's the matter, Rosie?" he said, looking puzzled. He knew it wasn't normal for me not to be upset over missing out on a night of baseball.

"Nothin'," I said.

As I gladly put the thoughts of having to deal with Coach Ski that evening out of my mind, Sleepy turned to me and raised his eyebrows. My eyes remained fixed on the baseball game on television. In a flash, the runner was off for the steal.

"Look at him go!" I said.

Sleepy's eyes turned toward the television. Within a few seconds, he forgot all about me not caring about practice.

Chapter Eight

It rained for two long days. Every five minutes I changed my mind about the all-star team. At one point, I called out for my mother to explain everything. I was going to tell her how much I hated the way Coach Ski treated me. How he didn't want me. How nobody cared.

"What, Rosa?" she said as she looked up from her magazine.

I stopped. Suddenly I felt like a wimp. *It was only one practice. Maybe he would lighten up. I guess I never gave him a chance. I'll go to the game and see what happens.*

"Forget it," I mumbled.

On Saturday afternoon, colorful teams of kids brought life back to the soggy, lonely fields. I confidently jogged through our warm-ups figuring that we all would receive equal playing time. This was an all-star team, which meant everybody was supposed to be good. And we were all 11 years old – it was supposed to be fun.

But not this team. Not with this rotten coach. I played a grand total of three innings during both games, which gave me all the time on the bench I needed to take back the second chance I gave Coach Ski. In the last inning of the first game, he took

Fishbone out, and stuck me in the lonesome right field.

All I could do was watch my father tear up his own path in the dirt and grass behind the backstop. His clenched fists were jammed in his pockets. He looked out at me in right field. I felt useless, forgotten. I returned to the same dreadful position later in the second game, and received the same amount of action I did in the first: none.

We collected our first two victories, but it wasn't easy. Nick and Ryan played well as usual, and Sleepy held his own at the catcher's spot. But Luke, Vic, and Fish each struck out twice, and even the smooth-talking Cowboy struggled at the plate.

"Knock us in, Rosie," Cowboy muttered to me after he struck out. I nodded my head. As I kicked the dirt around in the batter's box, I heard a helmet clang against the fence. I turned over my shoulder with wide eyes. All of us were a bit surprised at Cowboy's temper.

"I can't hit!" he yelled.

"Don't worry about it, Cowboy," Sleepy said. "You'll get it next time."

Cowboy quickly scooped up his helmet and bat, and put them in their proper places.

Every time I stepped up to the plate that day, I heard Sleepy cheering unusually loud for me. Of course he couldn't compete with my mother. Her chants buried all those coming from the dugout.

"Hammer away, Rosa!" she shouted. "Hammer away!"

On one hit, I smacked a ball that landed between center and right, which gave me a triple. Luke followed me up to bat, and in three pitches he sat back down again. It was our third out. As I jogged back in the dugout, I thought of how little my triple did for the team. I listened to Coach Ski reel off names and positions for the next inning. When I didn't hear mine, I dropped my helmet down and headed to the bench, where I sat for the rest of the game.

"Nice game," Cowboy said later as we were gathering our belongings. "You blasted that triple. Where'd you get all that power?"

I shrugged my thin shoulders. He was trying to make me feel better. But it didn't work. I felt even worse. I walked over to where my parents had set their lawn chairs. Rico tipped the bill of my hat over my face. I pulled it off and flipped it backwards.

"Way to hit the ball, kid," he said. I couldn't even look him in the eye. My mother fidgeted with my long braid as Sleepy walked up next to me. I needed to laugh or else I was gonna cry.

"You both were wonderful," she said.

"You were more wonderful," Sleepy joked as he looked at me. I looked at him and grinned.

My father was off chatting with Luke's father. Luke didn't play much either, so I'm sure they had a lot to talk about. My father broke from the conversation and joined us as we walked to our cars.

"Close games," he said as I grew nervous. "I don't think the coaches are too happy about it. There's a lot of pressure to win it all this year."

I tried not to look directly at him. One discouraged look from me would disturb him enough to go right over and say something about my lack of playing time. But it was too late. He knew how much it hurt a kid who loved baseball as much as I did to be riding the pine.

"I'll be back in a moment," my father grumbled.
"No, Dad," I begged as I tugged on his arm.
"Please don't say anything. Please."

"Don't worry, Rosie," he assured me. "I'm just going to ask him why he's playing you for only three innings of a double header."

"No," I pleaded. "It will make it worse."

Every kid knew what a disaster things became when parents started screaming over positions and playing time.

"Give him one more game," Rico said. "She's got to wait it out."

"It's not fair," my dad said shaking his head.

"Give it time," Rico said calmly. "She'll prove herself. Coaches don't like it when you walk on their turf and tell them what they should be doing."

"I won't tell him anything," my stubborn dad replied.

"Please, Jimmy," my mother hushed. "Let it go for today."

I held my breath. I looked up at Sleepy, who was staring uncomfortably at the ground.

"Hang in there, Rosie," I heard a voice say. I turned and it was Doc walking with his son, Fishbone. "If it's the last thing I do on this team, I will see to it that you're given a fair shot."

Fishbone's pretty blue eyes sparkled underneath his Slugger's cap and his tiny round mouth didn't move. He didn't say much around adults either, and we both knew that now wasn't the time to talk. There was a long pause.

"Thank you," said my mother, who like all of us, was a bit taken back by Doc's promising words. My father added his thanks as he watched Doc slip into his car and reach over to unlock the door for his son.

Rico patted me on the back. "Why don't you two ride with me?" he asked.

"Can we, Ma?" I asked.

"Go ahead," she said. "We'll order pizza when you get home."

Rico, Sleepy, and I walked through the maze of cars together.

"You all right, kid?" he asked just loud enough for me to hear. I nodded my head feeling a little better after hearing what Doc had to say.

"My agent called me last night," Rico said in a calm voice.

"Really?" I replied. "What'd he say?"

"There might be a spot for me on a Triple A team. I'll know within a couple of weeks."

"Wow," I said in awe.

"But promise me that you won't say anything to Mom and Dad about it. You neither, Sleep," he added as he looked at Sleepy, whose ears had picked up on the good news. "I just don't want Mom getting her hopes up, and praying for me all hours of the day. And Dad..."

His voice trailed off. He didn't have to say why he didn't want Dad to find out. I learned through Rico's numerous attempts at making it in the pros that there was a huge risk with every decision. Nothing was guaranteed. And the worst thing that Rico would have to deal with is hearing more negative things from my father if things didn't work out again.

"I won't tell anyone," I promised. "We can talk about it with each other, right?" I looked at Sleepy who was smiling.

"All right," Rico said. "But if I find out one of you told someone, you'll both be my personal ball girl and ball boy for life."

"We already are," I said with a grin. Rico wrapped his arms around me and threw me over his shoulder. Sleepy playfully punched him in the stomach in his effort to rescue me.

It felt good to laugh. And it felt even better to hear something good about someone else. But the good news didn't last long.

Chapter Nine

"**C**ome on, Rosie," Coach Ski snapped. "Get your body in front of it."

Two hits later, he nailed another shot at me. It was far beyond my reach.

"We're not going to win state if we play like that!" he called out.

Why am I here? I chased after the ball and picked it up. Then I furiously fired the ball back into Doc. *Do something!* He did nothing. *That's it. Nobody wants me. So, fine. This is the last one.*

Later as we jogged into the dugout, I watched my teammates closely. I was looking for any sign that they were feeling as awful as I was. But they continued to laugh and joke around. Even Sleepy did, too. It hurt me even more to see that they were having so much fun. *Why can't I?*

"Hey batta, batta, swing batta!" Vic yelled to Joe as he stepped up to the plate.

"Ride it on outta here!" Cowboy shouted. "Give him the heat, Coach Ski. I dare you."

Joe swung and barely got a hold of the ball. It dribbled to the third baseman, who quickly threw Joe out.

"Let's go!" Luke hollered from left field after Joe grounded out. "That was too easy."

Ryan stepped up to plate next.

"Try and hit it to me Ry-ski!" Luke continued jeering. "Or are you Nick-Ski?"

"That's Ryan, right?" I asked Cowboy quietly as we leaned against the fence in the dugout. We both looked over at the other twin sitting at the end of the bench. He was wearing a batting glove.

"Yep," Cowboy said. *Crack!* Ryan's ball went smoking past the center fielder's head.

"That's Ryan, all right," Cowboy muttered.

It seemed that part of being a twin meant that one was constantly being compared to the other. Almost everybody in the league did it when they talked about the Samanski twins. Sleepy and I heard the rumors people were spreading – things like Nick making the all-star team because his father was the coach; and that nobody could really tell him apart from Ryan, who was the real superstar. I really didn't pay much attention at all, especially knowing the things people said about me, but I had a hunch that those rumors always swirled around in Nick's head.

Cowboy walked down to the end of the bench.

"Can I borrow your batting glove, Nick?" he asked. "I've been struggling, and I think it might help."

Nick sat biting his nails. He eyes dropped beneath his cap. "I don't know," he mumbled.

Cowboy stuck his open hand out and said, "I'll give it right back."

Nick took his fingertips out of his mouth and reluctantly tore the strap loose. He pulled off his lucky glove and slapped it into Cowboy's hand.

"Thanks, man," Cowboy said. He gritted his teeth and winced as he pulled it on. "All right," he added with a smile. "It's a little tight. But it will do. This one is for you, pal."

He gave Nick a sly wink. Nick smiled nervously as Cowboy strutted off to the plate. After two easy practice swings, he set himself in the batter's box, and smashed the first pitch Doc delivered. He dropped his bat and beat his feet down the base path.

"It's gotta be the glove," Cowboy yelled to Nick after he stopped at his spot on second base. Nick laughed out loud. I turned to him and smiled.

Vic stepped up to hit next. He bunted the second pitch, which moved Cowboy to third. Then it was Nick's turn up to bat. He hurried out of the dugout, and ran to third base, hoping to get his glove back from Cowboy.

"Let's go, Nick," Coach Ski shouted. "We don't have all day and we can't do that in the game."

Cowboy squeezed and twisted, but he could not pull the glove off.

"Go ahead," Cowboy mumbled as his eyes shifted nervously toward Coach Ski. "Before you get in trouble. I'll get it off later."

Nick moped away with a scowl on his face. When his father screamed, "Hustle!" Nick lifted his heavy feet up off the ground and dragged his bat to home plate.

I watched him carefully. I thought that maybe I wasn't the only one who was miserable. I stood up from my regular position on the bench, opened my mouth, and cheered for the first time.

"Hit away, Nick!" I yelled.

Sleepy turned and raised his eyebrows. "What's gotten into you all of a sudden?" he asked.

"Knock it outta here, Nick!" I yelled. Sleepy just shook his head. "You can do it!" I added.

Nick snapped his bat around and foul tipped a grounder. He frowned as he looked down the third base line. With his hand on his hip, he glared at Cowboy and begged for his glove back. But Cowboy ignored him.

"You can do it, Nick-Ski!" Cowboy shouted encouragingly. "Just like I taught ya."

"I can't," Nick complained. "I need my glove."

"No, you don't," Cowboy yelled back. "You can hit it with your eyes closed."

Nick's worried face finally broke into a tentative smile. His body relaxed, and he took a deep breath to regain his focus.

Pow! He smashed a shot that hit the centerfield fence. It was further than Ryan's hit, even though I quickly reminded myself that I really shouldn't be comparing the two. It was just a great hit – easily the best hit by anyone that evening. I watched Nick as he rounded third. He thought about heading for home, but he stopped and retreated safely. As he tipped his helmet up, his face turned red.

"Way to go, Nick-Ski!" Cowboy bellowed as he ran up the third base line after crossing home plate. Then he threw his shoulders back and wound up for one big chest butt. Nick gladly accepted the thumping, and we all cheered wildly.

I stepped up to plate and connected for a single. As I stood on first base, I looked over to Doc. He gave me the steal sign. I dashed for second base and easily beat the throw. Ryan caught the ball and pushed his glove into me, almost knocking me off the base. I fell back, but kept a toe on the white cushion.

"You've got to be tougher than that out there, Rosie!" Coach Ski yelled from home plate.

"Yeah," Ryan said. "No girls allowed on this field."

I turned to him with fire in my eyes and said, "Then get off."

I couldn't believe the words came out of my mouth, but when they did, I was glad.

Cowboy just about fell over laughing at shortstop.

"She told you!" he yelled.

Sleepy and Joe laughed loudly. My words shocked Ryan so much that he stood there speechless. Then like a tidal wave, his emotions came to the surface. His lip quivered, his fists clenched and he bolted after me. I darted away, bobbing and weaving around in the outfield grass. I wasn't scared or worried about Ryan catching me. I was having too much fun turning him into a screaming, angry mess.

"Stop, Ryan!" Nick screamed. "Stop!"

Ryan sucked in air as he pumped his arms and ran even faster. Sleepy and Cowboy finally caught up to us.

"Ryan!" Cowboy hollered. "Stop!"

"You can't catch her, anyway," Sleepy called out proudly.

"Yeah, I can," Ryan insisted.

"Rosie and Ryan!" a voice boomed. Coach Ski marched out on the field with his fists clenched, his face red. "Take five laps around the field. Now!"

Coach Ski was gritting his teeth, and sputtering all over the place. I turned with my head held high and started jogging. I embarrassed him and his superstar son in front of the whole team, and was quite proud of myself. It wasn't anything personal against

Ryan. He said what was going through his mind, which was much more than his father would admit.

Ryan started gaining on me as we jogged around the field. All I could hear was each of us breathing. *I'm not apologizing. He should be the one to say he's sorry.* The tension grew with every step we took. He tried to pick up his speed, but I wouldn't let him pass me.

"What lap are we on?" he gasped.

I took a second to decide whether or not I would respond. I considered his speaking to me as the closest thing to an apology I would ever get.

"Four," I said.

Everything blew over once we returned to the field. Within five minutes, Cowboy started goofing off, and Coach Ski started screaming at him too.

"Stop horsing around!" Coach Ski called out. "I'm tired of this. That's it. Everybody go get some water."

After our break, Doc split us into teams for a scrimmage. I was up first. I cracked a single and then stole second base – the same base Ryan was covering.

"I dare you to steal," Ryan whispered. "You'll never make it."

I turned and my eyes locked into his, furious that he insisted upon testing me again. I waited until he dropped his glare. He did. I grabbed my knees tightly and set my foot on the corner of the base. I turned and studied Joe's movement on the pitcher's mound. When Joe let the ball go, it was like the chains that had been holding me back had finally snapped. I was free. Gone in a flash. Nobody could touch me. I was Rosie Cool Mama Jones.

The ball was thrown too late, and I made it safely to third. "Hold it!" Coach Ski roared and he stomped onto the field. I thought he was going to yell at Sleepy for not making the throw fast enough. But then Coach Ski turned to me. "I didn't give you a sign, did I?"

I hid my eyes under my helmet and braced myself.

"What do you think you are doing? Who do you think you are?" Coach Ski yelled harshly. "No one — and I repeat, *no one,* is allowed to steal unless we give you the sign."

I rolled my eyes and rested my hands on my hips. I just couldn't do anything right.

"Do you have a problem, young lady?" Coach Ski yelled.

I stared right through his steely eyes. Some rotten names were at the tip of my tongue, but I said nothing. If I did, he would have thrown me off the team. And I didn't want to give him the satisfaction of humiliating me any more than he already had.

Fortunately, practice ended 10 minutes later. I jumped into a full sprint at the sight of Rico's car. He pulled up just in time. I was on the verge of bursting into one of those rare, long, exhausting sobs. I had to get off the field, and get Coach Ski out of my sight.

"How was practice?" Rico asked as Sleepy and I piled our gear into his car.

Sleepy's eyes fell upon me, and he waited for me to answer my brother's question. I shrugged my shoulders. "It was all right," I replied.

Rico turned to Sleepy, who rolled his eyes and shook his head.

"You wanna talk about it?" Rico asked.

"No," I grumbled.

"You sure?" my brother tried again.

"Everything is fine," I said calmly.

Rico eyed me suspiciously, and then dropped the subject.

• • • •

My problems didn't end on the baseball field that week. On Friday night, I couldn't do anything right at our basketball game either. We played horribly and lost. Mr. O'Malley and Mr. Harris let us hear it afterwards.

"You're not playing the way you're capable of," Mr. O'Malley's voice boomed. We all stared at the ground until he was finished.

"Penny," Wil whispered as we broke from our huddle, "you think we can go out for pizza still?"

"I don't know," Penny said and she shrugged.

"What about a sleep-over?" Wil asked.

Penny turned to Molly. "Go ask," Penny said.

"Why do I always have to ask?" grumbled Molly.

"Just do it," Angel said. "Who cares? It's your dad."

"Yeah, but he's mad because we lost."

"Just go do it."

"Fine," she muttered, "I hope he doesn't yell."

We all pretended not to be looking as we shot the balls up at the basket. I peeked over my shoulder and caught Molly walking back to us.

"So?" Penny whispered anxiously.

"He said yes," Molly simply said, and then she grinned.

"All right!" Wil shrieked. Her pudgy, smiling cheeks nudged her glasses up on her face. "I'll bring over some brownies I made today. That's if no one found them in my secret hiding spot."

We went straight to the O'Malley's house and called our parents for permission to spend the night.

My father answered the phone. "Dad, can I please stay overnight at Molly's?"

"Well, you've got another double header tomorrow."

"Please, Dad," I said softly. "The game isn't until eleven."

"I don't think it's a good idea. You need your rest."

"Come on, Dad," I begged.

"No, Rosie. How about I come pick you up at 10:30?" he proposed. "You can have your fun, but I think you should get a good night's rest."

I huffed and then sighed knowing his mind was made up. Begging and whining would have been embarrassing in front of all my friends. "Fine," I finally said.

I got off the phone and broke the news to the Ballplayers.

"You can't stay?" Wil asked in disbelief.

"No," I said sadly. "I've got a game tomorrow. It's not like it matters, anyway," I mumbled.

"What do you mean, it doesn't matter?" asked Penny.

I shrugged my shoulders. I knew I slipped. I didn't want anyone to hear me gripe about practice or playing time. I didn't want anyone to find out if I decided not to play anymore. I just wasn't sure yet, and I knew nobody would understand.

"I heard those twins are really good," Molly said.

I breathed a sigh of relief. The change of subject took the pressure off me. "Yeah," I said. "They are."

"Who's better?" Wil asked.

"I don't know," I said. "Nick's quiet, but Ryan's kind of cocky. He bugs me sometimes. But they're both good. And most of us can't tell them apart anyway. Nick wears a batting glove. That's the only way I can tell."

"I heard that their father is just plain nuts," Wil said. "He makes them get up in the morning and throw and run. And if they don't play well, he punishes them and doesn't let them hang out with their friends."

"I never heard that," I said. I was surprised by the rumors. I couldn't imagine having to put up with a father like that.

"That would be awful," moaned Angel.

"That kid named Cowboy is on your team, isn't he?" Molly asked.

"Yeah," I said.

"What's he like?" asked Penny.

"Uh-huh. Yeah," Wil smiled mischievously. "You got a thing for Cowboy. Don't ya, P?"

Penny clicked her tongue and tried to hide her smile. Although I didn't have any heartaches over any boys yet, even I saw right through Penny.

"What's he like, Rosie?" Molly repeated.

"He's nice," I said. "Everybody likes him."

"You got his phone number?" Angel teased.

Penny clicked her tongue again. "You are making this up. Even Rosie said it — he's nice. There's nothing to talk about."

"Where's your game tomorrow, Rosie?" Wil asked.

"Tucker Park."

"We might have to stop by," she said.

"Hold up," Penny said. "I'm not going to a baseball game to watch a boy. I go to watch Rosie."

"Uh-huh," Wil said grinning.

"Now you're all gonna think that the only reason I would want to go is to see him," Penny said, "and that's not right."

"We know," Molly said confidently, "but it doesn't mean that we're going to stop teasing you."

"We'll be there," Wil said and she looked right at me.

I didn't smile. My insides ached. All my friends were coming to watch me sit on the bench. I tried to think of a way to tell them that I wasn't going, but I couldn't.

Chapter Ten

The public humiliation continued on Saturday when I played a total of four innings in two games. After the second game as the crowd cleared, my father walked right up to Coach Ski. Coach Ski stood silently as my father spoke slowly and clearly. I stood in the parking lot without any feeling at all. I just didn't care anymore. I hated playing on that lousy team.

My father finished what he had to say. He turned away from Coach Ski and walked over to the car with his head down. He stopped in front of me and looked me in the eyes.

"Why didn't you tell me about what happened in practice this week?" my father asked.

"What?" I gasped.

"Coach Samanski said that you started fighting with Ryan," he explained.

I suddenly felt weak. I could not make myself believe that Coach Ski made up such a story. *What is he trying to do to me?*

"I didn't do anything," I pleaded. When my father's expression did not change, I knew right then that Coach Ski had him convinced.

"Ryan started it," I mumbled.

Then I realized what I had just done and wanted to take my words back. I had admitted that I did something when I hadn't done anything. Nothing I said would make a difference anyway. Adults always believe adults. Even unfair adults like Coach Ski. I felt my temperature rise, and all the anger came pouring out of me.

"I didn't do anything!" I shouted.

"I'm disappointed in you, Rosa," my father said.

His voice faded. I couldn't believe it. My own father thought his only daughter, who hardly said a word unless spoken to, had picked a fight with the coach's son. The tears welled up in my eyes. I turned to my mother, and my pleading eyes begged for her understanding. Her unsure eyes shifted back to my father.

"Let's all get in the car and talk about this at home," she said.

I started walking away. I didn't want to go home to parents who didn't trust me. I didn't want to see my lousy brother who wasn't even there when I needed him. I made up my mind that I would go to a pay phone and call Sleepy's mother. She'd let me live with her family.

"Rosie, come back here!" my father's voice boomed.

I kept my eyes on the ground and started running. I heard my father grunting as he pounded his feet on the ground behind me. I swiftly turned the corner and headed down Maxwell. When people started to stare at the scene we were making, my father stopped. I kept running.

I slowed down when I reached the corner of Maxwell and Woodside. Just as I turned up Woodside,

I heard a car's engine by my side. I looked over my shoulder. My mother rolled down the window and leaned out.

"Have you cooled off, yet, Rosa?" she asked as the car moved alongside of me.

I turned my eyes ahead and kept running.

"Please get in the car," she said.

I ignored her.

"Rosa," her voice commanded me to get in the car or else. I knew that if she came after me, she would have caught me, and spanked me like a child, and my mother's spankings always hurt. I slowed down to a fast walk and glanced inside the car.

"Where is he?" I asked.

"I made him walk," my mother replied. "He needed to cool off, too. Please get in the car."

I turned and took two steps toward the moving vehicle. She stopped and I got in the back seat. I refused to speak. So my mother used the fill-in-the-blank, question-and-answer session to piece together everything.

"You didn't do anything, did you?"

"No," I said. "You can ask Sleepy."

"Fine," she said. "I believe you. Now why are you so upset?"

What a stupid question. Is she blind? Did she imagine that she saw her daughter playing in the games? How could she not know?

I crossed my arms across my chest and said nothing.

"Some things in life are not easy," she said. "You have to decide what makes you happy. No one else can do that for you. If playing on this team with this coach is too hard for you to handle, you don't have to do it."

What? I could not believe that my mother was giving me permission to quit.

"When I pick up your father, you have to tell him what has been going on," she said, "or else we will never know what is hurting you."

She had turned around to track down my father. I hid my eyes under my cap as he grabbed the handle and opened the door. He grunted as he sat down in the seat. He turned around and yelled at me, "You're grounded, young lady!"

"Why don't you listen to her for once?" my mother said bitterly. "Ask her what happened."

"I really don't think Coach Samanski would just make it all up," he told her.

"Rosalinda," my mother said, "tell your father what happened."

I didn't lift my eyes up. I stared down at my *coquí* charm hanging from my glove, and just started talking.

"Ryan said no girls are allowed on the field. So I told him to get off. He didn't like it, so he came running after me, and Coach Ski started screaming at both of us. It was no big deal."

The car fell silent. I heard my father take a deep breath, and then I caught my mother's eyes in the rear view mirror. She was grinning proudly.

"I'm sorry," my father said softly.

I stared out the window and let go of all of my frustration and fear. Not only did my father finally listen to me, but he actually seemed proud of me standing up for myself.

"Coach Samanski said that if you do well in practice this week," my father added, "you'll definitely play
next weekend."

I wanted to cry all over again. *Couldn't he be proud
of me for more than 30 seconds? Didn't he understand what
kind of guy we were dealing with? Coach Ski isn't going to
play me. He is too busy looking for excuses. I don't want to
ever see him again.*

"She doesn't have to play anymore if she doesn't
want to," my mother said.

"Yes, she does," my father replied. "I didn't raise
her to be a quitter."

"We, you mean," my mother said, correcting him.
They started arguing again. I don't know who had
the last word. When we arrived at the house, I went
straight to my room.

● ● ● ●

The next day, Rico took me to the cages. When
he asked me what happened after the game, I looked
away from him. I just wanted to forget about the whole
embarrassing incident.

"Dad is always going to be tough on us," he said.
"Mama tells me that it's the only way he can show us
that he cares. It makes me really mad sometimes. I
just don't know if I will ever understand it."

"Neither do I," I grumbled.

"What did Mama tell you to do?" he asked.

"She said I didn't have to play if I didn't want to,"
I said.

When Rico smiled, I just gave up trying to understand my family.

"She knows what's going through your head more than you think she does," he said. "What are you going to do?"

I shrugged and then lifted my bat up to my shoulder. I turned my focus on the machine in front of me and started swinging.

• • • •

For three days, I thought about what I should do. By Tuesday night, I had made a decision not to go. Then I changed my mind again right before practice.

I watched as the ball skipped across the matted grass in our small front yard. I walked over and slowly crouched my body down. As I stood up, I pulled the ball out with my right hand, and lazily side-armed a throw back to Sleepy. His chubby cheeks grinned as he scooped up his grounder.

"Throw me some line drives!" he called out. "Then some pop flies."

I dragged myself through the motions. After I fumbled the next three catches, he stopped and stared me down.

"What's the matter, Rosie?" Sleepy asked.

"Nothin'," I said as I shrugged my shoulders.

"You sick?" he asked.

I paused before I answered, thinking it would have been a good excuse, but I couldn't lie to my best friend. I shook my head.

"You've been acting weird," Sleepy said. "What's wrong?"

"Nothin'," I shot back.

"You like the all-stars?" he asked.

My eyes looked at the ground. "Yeah," I mumbled.

"Doesn't look like it," he said. "Is Ryan still buggin' you?"

I shook my head.

"Then what's wrong?" he asked.

I didn't answer.

"Something's gotta be wrong with you," Sleepy huffed in frustration. "You look like you don't even care anymore. You can tell me, Rosie. I won't say a word. I promise."

I could tell by the serious look in his eyes that there was no getting out of this one.

"It's not you or anybody on the team," I began. "It's..."

"Coach Ski," Sleepy said. "I know."

"He doesn't like me," I blurted out.

"No," Sleepy said. "He just can't stand a girl being able to play. Everyone on the team knows it."

That was news to me. I didn't think anyone else cared about what was going on.

"I can't stand him," I mumbled. "He's always gonna think I'm not good enough. I hate practice, and I hate the games."

"You're not thinking of quitting are you?"

When I shrugged my shoulders, Sleepy's eyes grew wide.

"I'm never gonna play," I tried to explain. "It's all for nothing."

Sleepy's mouth dropped open. "You can't quit," he said. "If you did you'd just be proving him right. And what are people going to say? Oh, yeah, that Rosie Jones girl – she quit. What am I gonna say when people ask me where you are? That you quit?"

Hearing those words hurt. But worse than that was seeing how much I disappointed Sleepy. He stared off in the distance, shaking his head.

A horn blared. I turned and watched Rico's car roll into our driveway.

"What are you doing home?" I asked my brother as he stepped out of the car. "Aren't you supposed to be working?"

He shook his head and said, "I came home early to take you to practice."

"Mama said she was taking us," I told him.

"I am," he said surely. "You two punks ready?"

Sleepy's serious eyes fell upon me. I stared right back at my best friend and smiled for the first time that afternoon.

"I got the front seat," I called out.

"No, you don't," Sleepy yelled, and he then darted for the other side of the car. I playfully smacked him on the back with my glove when he beat me to it.

Rico sat in his car for most of practice. I didn't look over to him much, but I was glad that he was there. Coach Ski divided us up into three groups and took turns working at three separate hitting stations. At one station, we practiced hitting against the fence. Our partner dropped the ball in front of the batter to quicken our reflexes. At the next station, we worked out with a doughnut weight on our bat as Doc came around checking our swings.

"Don't dip your shoulder, Rosie," he called. "Keep your head on the ball, Nick. Choke up, Sleep."

When the whistle blew, we rotated to the next station, where we practiced hitting live pitches from Ryan. Nick asked if he could practice his pitching, too.

"Not now," Coach Ski said. "A little later, maybe. Let Ryan get loosened up."

Nick walked away dejectedly.

"Sleepy!" Coach Ski yelled. "You're up. Rosie on deck. Nick on double deck. The rest of you in the field."

Each player received five pitches. Ryan unloaded all his strength on every pitch, and threw his fastballs right down the pipe. When Sleepy whiffed on two out of three, I knew that I was in for a true test of my hitting ability.

"He's throwin' smoke," Sleepy muttered as he passed me.

I stepped up to the plate and knocked the dirt off my cleats with my bat. I took the first pitch. It was high and outside, and flying so fast that I could hear it whiz by.

"Keep throwing the heat, Ry," Coach Ski said.

I took a deep breath and imagined myself in the batting cages with Rico. Then I took two practice swings and stepped back into the box. I swung hard at the next pitch and pulled the ball in the pocket between short and left field. *Nice one.* The third pitch I dipped under and flied out. *Keep your head on it. Don't dip that shoulder.* I cracked the fourth pitch to short. *You gotta get it out of the infield, kid.* I slammed the fifth to center field. *One more. Get this one!* With Coach Ski catching three feet behind me, I desperately wanted to erase all his doubts with one awesome stroke of the bat.

Ryan wound up and delivered the pitch. I swung so hard that I spun around and almost lost my helmet. I missed by a mile.

"Dipped the shoulder, Rosie," Coach Ski said. "Took your head right off it. I keep telling you that. Next batter up."

My heart sank. I missed my chance at hitting almost every pitch thrown by one of the best fastball pitchers in the state. I dropped my bat down and dragged it through the dirt. I peeked up at Rico, who was leaning up against the hood of his car. He nodded his head and winked. *Hang in there, kid.* I just shook my head.

When our scrimmage time came around, everyone begged positions they could play.

"You're all going to play everywhere," Coach Ski assured us. "So everybody just settle down."

I jogged to my assignment in the doldrums of right field. All the infield starters played their regular positions, which was a clear indication that Coach Ski's promise about rotating everyone didn't have much truth behind it.

Hardly anything ever happened out in right field. I could have jumped the fence and run down the street for a lemonade and no one would have noticed. It was killing me to be out there doing nothing. I needed something to keep my mind interested. So I quietly pretended I was an announcer just like Cowboy.

"Jackson up to bat, Samanski on the mound..." I muttered quietly.

I got bored after about five minutes. So I quietly sang songs, and occasionally mumbled some more awful things about Coach Ski.

"Look alive outfield!" Doc yelled. I knew he was talking to me, so I raced in to back up the first baseman on every throw. I couldn't afford to have Doc on my case, too.

The coaches each took turns at bat and had Sleepy and Joe run for them. On one series of hits and steals, Sleepy had worked his way around to third base. Cowboy jabbered to him from his shortstop position.

"Don't even think about stealing home, Sleep," he jeered. "We're just baiting you."

"That's enough, Cowboy!" Coach Ski snapped. "No more talking to the base runners."

Doc cracked a shot right at me. I shook my head and blinked my eyes once before my body reacted. I couldn't believe a hit was coming into my territory. I jerked forward and sprinted forward in a panic. I relaxed just in time to make the catch. My eyes automatically turned to third base, and I watched Sleepy head for home. I fired the ball perfectly to Luke who made the catch and tagged my friend out.

"Way to go, Rosie!" Doc exclaimed. I felt a cool rush of adrenaline and breathed a deep sigh of relief.

"Nice play," Coach Ski muttered. It was the only compliment that I had received from him in almost two weeks.

Two plays later, Coach Ski reprimanded Cowboy again for chatting with Fishbone on second base.

"How are we supposed to win if you can't act serious for more than five minutes?" Coach Ski screamed, and then there was a long pause.

"Cowboy, take right!" Doc hollered and he waved me in. "Come on in, Rosie. Take short."

My heart skipped a beat. I couldn't believe that Doc had gone right over Coach Ski and promoted me to the front line. I ran past Cowboy with my eyes on the ground, not knowing what to say.

"Jones to replace Cowboy at short," Cowboy cackled in a radio voice. "Well, folks. Let's see what the little lady's got."

I glared at him. I was tired of being singled out because I was a girl.

"OK, excuse me," Cowboy corrected himself. "Let's see what this kid's got."

I looked up and smiled.

Coach Ski substituted all the players and filled every position on the field. He and Doc took turns batting, and calling out the plays.

"Play's at first," Coach Ski said. He hit a hard grounder to Nick at second, and Nick fired a perfect throw to Ryan at first.

"Play's at second or first," Coach Ski yelled. He nailed a shot to Luke on third. Luke scooped the ball up and side-armed it to Nick at second base. Nick swiveled around, jumped and fired it to first base.

"Double Trouble for the double play!" Cowboy yelled from deep in right. Coach Ski glared at him, and Cowboy scooped his glove over his mouth.

"Heads up, infield!" Coach Ski yelled. Then he gave me one stern look, which meant the next ball was coming my way. He slammed a hard grounder. I jumped towards it and felt it slap in my glove. I then fired a perfect throw to first base. On the next two plays, he drilled me a line drive, and then a pop fly. I snagged both of them out of the air and fired the ball to the appropriate bases.

Coach Ski wiped his brow. Instead of skipping me this time, he tossed the ball up and gritted his teeth as he took one last shot. The ball looked as if it was going to split the seam between me at shortstop, and Luke at third. We both lunged for it. I extended my body and kept my eyes locked on the ball. The power of the hit pulled my glove back. I went down on one knee, popped up and turned for the throw. I knew when I let it go that Sleepy didn't have a chance.

"Atta way, kid!" Doc yelled after I threw my best friend out.

"Nothing gets by!" screamed Cowboy from deep in right field.

At the end of practice, Rico stepped out on the field to toss the ball around.

"If he doesn't play you on Saturday," Rico whispered as he passed me, "he's crazy." He winked and I smiled.

After practice, Sleepy convinced Cowboy, Fish, and even the twins to join us for a game of run the bases. Rico and Ryan tried to catch the rest of us as we sprinted madly from one base to the other. Sleepy and I gladly put ourselves in the pickle between two bases, and then danced and wiggled and faked our way out of it. Nick began to take more chances, too. He laughed and taunted all the players, especially Ryan.

"Come on, you wimp," Ryan yelled back at Nick. "You're not gonna make it. You're scared."

On the very next toss, Nick took off in a fury. He lost his footing and slipped. When he looked up, he realized that he was in a pickle there was no getting out of. Rico tossed the ball to Ryan just in time for him to make the catch and tag his brother. Ryan plucked the ball out of the air, reached down, and slapped Nick hard on the back with his glove.

"You jerk!" Nick screamed as he pulled himself up from the ground. His bottom lip quivered and he clenched his fists. "You didn't have to hit me so hard!"

"You're such a baby," Ryan muttered.

Nick's face flushed red with anger. "I'm not a baby. You're a baby." He lunged toward Ryan and tackled him. The twins flailed around on the ground, kicking and punching each other. We waited a few seconds for them to stop, but they didn't. Rico hustled over and pulled the two apart.

"Settle down, guys," Rico said as he tried to restrain Nick. Both of them caught their breaths, and bent down to pick up their caps.

Coach Ski, who only saw the tail end of the fight, stormed over. His mouth tensed into an angry line. "What's the problem?"

"It just got a little competitive," Rico said.

"Nick tackled me because he got mad when I tagged him out!" Ryan cried out.

"He punched me with his glove!" Nick exclaimed, and the tears flooded his eyes.

"What did I tell you two about fighting?" Coach Ski said bitterly. "Go and sit in the car. The both of you. Don't let me catch you fighting or arguing again."

His harsh words slammed the conversation shut. Ryan and Nick trudged to their car without speaking. The rest of us stood still for a few seconds, waiting for someone to say or do something other than stare wide-eyed at everyone else. Coach Ski finally turned and walked away. Cowboy scooped up the ball and tossed it to Sleepy.

"Looks like Double Trouble is in real trouble now," Cowboy said quietly.

Chapter Eleven

Sleepy turned the handle on the gray iron gate. "I'll race you to center field," he said.

"To where?" I asked as I stepped into the ballpark.

"The 215 sign," he said as he pointed out past the freshly chalked lines of the dirt infield. I dropped my glove, and took off for a head start.

"That's cheating!" Sleepy blurted out just as he jumped into a sprint.

The head start gave me just enough room to beat him to the fence. I slapped the 215 sign with the palm of my hand, and then turned to Sleepy.

"That's right," he breathed heavily, "you need a head start to beat me."

I brushed off his comment. "Race you back?" I proposed.

He bent over and grabbed his knock-knees as he panted. I wasn't sure if he heard me, so I repeated, "Sleepy, I'll race..."

I blinked and he was gone. The smiling sneak tricked me into thinking he was resting. Before I could finish what he had obviously already heard, my body jolted forward to catch him. But I couldn't make up for his head start no matter how hard I tried.

"Call me 'Cool Papa'," Sleepy said with a pearly grin.

I laughed as we both gasped for air. I looked up and watched as family and friends set their lawn chairs behind our dugout. Others began to fill the small section of wooden bleachers. I saw Mr. Martino with his daughter on his hip. She waved to me.

"Go get 'em, Rosie!" he yelled. I smiled and waved my glove back.

"Take me out to the ball game," Cowboy bellowed as we warmed up. "Take me out to the crowd..."

"Let's go, Sluggers!" my mom hollered.

I began to block out the cheers, and started thinking about the game. I imagined myself at short-stop, scooping up all the balls hit to me, and making perfect throws to first base just like I did at practice. Then I saw myself walking up to the plate and smack-ing the ball with ease just like I did with Rico in the batting cages. My mind could hear the crowd roar-ing. I could feel the excitement.

Then out of nowhere, a dark shadow of despair clouded my high hopes. I couldn't avoid thinking about how little I had played in all the previous games. I began to consider the possibility of spending an-other afternoon on the bench.

"Hustle in, guys!" Doc hollered.

His voice snapped me out of my daze. We all went charging into the dugout. I eagerly awaited my as-signment.

"Nick at second, Ryan's on the mound," Coach Ski began. "Luke on third. Cowboy take short. Rosie, you're in right."

A bunch of muddled up feelings ran through me as I hustled out of the dugout. I wanted so badly to play short. Then I quickly reminded myself that right field was a lot better than being left out.

"Who's got a ball?" yelled Vic.

I hustled back and grabbed a ball from under the bench. My eyes awkwardly stopped at Fishbone, who usually played right field. I hid my eyes under my cap as I scurried past him. Doc slapped me on the back as I took the field.

"Let's go, Rosie!" he shouted.

As every inning passed, I wondered if it would be my last. I was so worried about playing that I lost all my concentration. In the third inning I swung so hard at a pitch, I had to catch myself from falling down.

"Just meet it, Rosie," Doc yelled.

But I didn't listen. I felt the anxiety to do something big, like smack a dinger that Coach Ski wouldn't forget. I foul tipped for strike two, and then whiffed again on the next pitch.

"Strike three," the umpire called out.

The crowd moaned in disappointment, and then they began to whisper. I dejectedly walked back to the dugout knowing what they were saying. *She isn't tough enough. She isn't good enough. Girls shouldn't be playing on the all-star team.*

I ended up spending four consecutive innings with the sun beating directly on me in right field. During one inning, I pulled the bill of my cap down snugly trying to block the blinding rays. I turned to my left, and saw the Ballplayers. They had gathered by the right-field fence. Wil perked up and smacked Molly on the arm when she saw me look at her.

"Hey, Rosie!" Wil yelled. I smiled, and quickly returned to my ready position.

Out of the corner of my eye, I caught Molly's reluctant wave. She then turned to Penny and muttered

something. I was sure they were talking about my being stuck in right field. My face felt hot and I felt a
rush of tears. I tipped my head down, swallowed hard
and held all my emotions inside.

The next batter cracked one solid. I could tell by
his feet and swing that his hit was coming straight at
me. I looked up in the air, and began to backpedal. I
kept my eye on the tiny white blur as it grew closer to
me. I was right under it when the ball disappeared in
the sun's blinding path. My eyes squinted and I
flinched. I heard the ball drop against the dirt and
looked down. I scooped the ball out of the grass and
fired it in. When the play was finally dead, I returned
back to my position. The opposing team's fans roared
and my eyes fell to the ground. It was all my fault. I
missed the big catch.

At the end of the inning, I jogged in, and sat down
on the bench next to Sleepy.

"Nice try," he said. "Did the sun get you?"

I shrugged my shoulders.

"I hate when that happens," he said.

"Rosie," Doc yelled. "Nice try. That one was near
impossible though. With or without the sun, it would
have been tough." He winked at me. "Keep your head
up."

At the end of the same inning, Coach Ski called
out substitutions.

"John," called Coach Ski. "You take right."

Fishbone jumped up and joined the outfielders
as they jogged out onto the dirt. I pushed my back up
against the dugout wall knowing that I was done for
the day. Then I turned to the Ballplayers again.

Wil waved and giggled, but this time her smile
did not stay. Molly looked at me and rolled her eyes.

Penny raised her eyebrows and shrugged her shoulders. I took a deep breath and looked off in the distance staring at nothing, but thinking about everything.

While I was on the bench, I paid close attention to how Coach Ski treated everyone else. In one inning, Cowboy let three stoppable balls pass him by.

"Get in front of it, Cowboy," Coach Ski said calmly.

But Cowboy didn't come out.

When Joe missed an easy catch in center, Coach Ski called out, "Shake it off, Joe."

But Joe didn't come out either.

I couldn't stand watching it anymore. I dropped my head down and fidgeted with my *coquí* charm. *I don't have any luck. Nothing is going right. This isn't fair.*

A piece of ice bounced off my shoulder, and I looked up. Luke was grinning devilishly. I scooped a handful of cubes out of the cooler and I retaliated. Within seconds, pieces of ice were flying all over the place.

"Stop horsing around!" Coach Ski scolded us.

I didn't care. When he turned his back, I threw another piece of ice. Coach Ski glared over his shoulder again. I fixed my bold eyes on him. *What are you gonna do? Bench me?*

"That's enough!" he screamed.

I dropped my head down and hid my smile under my cap. About a half hour later, we wrapped up and won the second game.

As we all walked to the parking lot, Cowboy said, "Good game."

I felt stupid. *Why is he saying good game? I didn't do anything.*

"I need a cool down," Sleepy said and he handed me his jug of water.

I twisted off the cap and poured the water all over Sleepy's head as he bent over. He stuck his tongue out to catch the running water.

Rico leaned over the fence. "Feel better, Sleepy?" he asked.

"Yep," Sleepy said and he grinned.

"I've gotta run," Rico said as he looked at me. "I'll talk to you later tonight, all right?"

I nodded my head. Then I thought of trying to deal with my father without Rico around. "Please stay, Rico," I begged.

"It will be all right," he said softly as he turned over his shoulder. He winked at me and then jogged away.

I walked up to my parents. Strangely enough, my father was sitting in a chair. My mother grabbed me by the hip and gave me a hug. Then I turned to my father. He muttered "good game" and stared blankly ahead. The back of his neck had turned beet-red from the sun. When I noticed how quiet he was, I crossed my fingers and hoped that he wouldn't go over to Coach Ski and blow up in front of all the other parents. I watched nervously as my father walked to our car, put the chairs in the trunk, and waited for me to finish talking with the Ballplayers. He stood all by himself and did not speak to anyone. I jogged over to the car and hopped in the back seat with Sleepy.

"You sick, Dad?" I asked.

"No," he said lowly.

"You don't look right."

"Well, I'm not," he said as if he was truly hurt. "What they're doing to you isn't right. I just don't know what to do about it."

I didn't say anything and neither did anyone else. My father drove the car home without speaking at all. I wasn't sure if he was mad. He just looked really sad and hurt, just like I felt when I was standing all alone in right field.

• • • •

Later that night I met up with the Ballplayers on the corner of Broadway and Woodside.

"Hey, Rosie," said Penny, who sounded as positive as ever. "Good game today."

I shrugged my shoulders and mumbled, "Thanks."

"You would have had an awesome game if they let you play," grumbled Molly. "What is wrong with that guy?"

"I don't know," I said. I began to feel helpless all over again. Coach Ski, who didn't even care about me, was controlling a very important part of my life. My favorite sport wasn't fun anymore. Instead of being proud of talking about baseball, I was ashamed.

When I came home that night, I went straight to my room and picked up my book. Reading helped clear my mind. I heard a soft knock on the door. It was Rico.

"How ya doing, kid?" he asked.

"I'm just reading," I said.

"I can see that," he said. "But how are you doing?" I said nothing. I felt my emotions build in my chest, and then ride up my throat in a lump.

"You okay, kid?" he asked sincerely as he sat down on the bed next to me. He rested his hand on my back.

"Why can't I be like everyone else?" I began. "Why can't I be treated just the same?"

Rico hugged me, and I started to cry.

"If I didn't have this long ponytail and my name wasn't Rosie it wouldn't be like this," I continued as the tears flowed from my eyes. "I should have just cut my hair and said that I was Ralph or Roger."

I paused. Rico sat silently as I continued. "And now Dad is all upset. I've never seen him like he was today. He looked so sad. It hurts him, too. I know it does. It's all because Coach Ski hates me," I moaned.

"He doesn't hate you," Rico said.

"Does too," I shot back.

"He's beginning to see that he's been all wrong about you," Rico said. "Just hang in there."

"It's not that easy," I muttered.

"Nothing comes easy, Rosie," he said.

"Why can't I be like everyone else?" I repeated.

"Because you're not like everyone else. You're special, kid. There is nobody else like you."

That wasn't what I wanted to hear. All adults said that cheery stuff, and now Rico was talking just like them. *What a fool I am for crying in front of my brother.* I wiped away my tears and took one last sniffle.

"If I'm so special," I asked, "then how come this is happening to me?"

Rico gave me another hug. "You've got to believe that this will all work out, Rosie," he said softly. "Just wait and you will see."

I laid down on my bed and buried my head in my pillow. I wanted to believe Rico, but I couldn't.

Chapter Twelve

Sleepy and I walked into the library on Tuesday morning and set our books on the counter.

"You finished those quickly," Ms. Daniel said with a smile. She tilted her head down and looked at me from behind her spectacles. "Are you looking for anything else in particular today?"

I shook my head. I was in no hurry to choose another book just yet. "I'm just going to look around," I said.

"Me, too," Sleepy agreed.

"Very well then," she said. "If you need any help, just let me know."

I smiled as I sat down at the magazine table, amazed by how cheerful Ms. Daniel always was. I started flipping through the stack of magazines sprawled over the table while Sleepy searched the card catalog.

"What are you getting, Sleep?" I whispered.

"I'm looking for something on Jackie Robinson," he said.

"Oh yeah," I said. "Good idea."

That reminded me about Rico asking me to pick up a book on Roberto Clemente. I looked through the index cards, found his name, and wrote down the call numbers. I followed the numbers on the bookshelves and stopped in front of the shelf I was looking for. I grew excited when I started pulling out all the books on Roberto.

I picked out two of the shorter ones, and skimmed the pages for a few minutes. I flipped and took a look at the black-and-white photos and read all the captions.

"What'd you get?" Sleepy asked as he leaned over my shoulder. I continued to stare at the pictures and read about all of Roberto's amazing accomplishments. A chill ran down my back when I read:

On December 31, 1972 Roberto Clemente flew to Nicaragua with supplies, medicine, and money. He wanted to help the earthquake victims there. Unfortunately, his airplane crashed into the sea. Rescuers never found Roberto's body.

"Rosie, what'd you get?" Sleepy asked again, louder.

"A book on Roberto," I whispered as I kept my eyes on the pages.

"You've got a lot of them there," Sleepy noticed.

I looked down at my pile. "I'm going to skim through," I said.

I still felt Sleepy's eyes on me. "Rosie, do you like coming to the library?" he asked.

I shrugged. I really didn't want to openly admit I enjoyed anything academic. "Do you?" I asked.

"Yeah," Sleepy said softly, "it's all right."

I didn't feel so bad after Sleepy said that he liked it, too. We read for a while, and then I gazed out the window. The sun was shining, and the sky was a bright blue. It was all too inviting to be sitting indoors.

"Let's go," I said, nudging Sleepy. He picked his head up from his book and looked at the clock.

"It's too early," he said. "We've got a half-an-hour left."

"Nerd," I kidded.

But Sleepy didn't find it amusing.

"Come on, Sleepy," I pleaded. "Nobody will find out and I'll read tonight."

Sleepy clicked his tongue and slammed his book shut. "All right," he muttered.

Just before we made it out the door, Ms. Daniel asked, "Leaving so soon?"

Sleepy and I stopped dead in our tracks and looked at each other.

"You usually stay for exactly two hours," she said, smiling. "Then you run out the door."

"Umm..." Sleepy said. "We just had to use the washroom."

We went out in the hallway, and I started laughing. Sleepy was shaking his head at first. Then his face finally broke into a wide grin.

"I told you we should have stayed, Rosie," he said.

"My dad probably called and asked her to watch us," I joked.

We stopped giggling and we each took a long drink at the water fountain. We wiped off our grins before we walked back into the library.

Sleepy made me stay an extra five minutes that day for trying to skip out earlier. I was mad at him for a while, but I got over it. After checking out our books and saying good-bye to Ms. Daniel, we rushed home for lunch. We played baseball and basketball at the park all afternoon. After dinner, we headed off to another night of all-star practice.

But it wasn't just another practice. It was the best night of the entire summer.

• • • •

I walked onto the field that night asking myself so many questions. *Why am I forcing myself to go through this? Am I doing this for me?*

No, I wasn't. I was doing it for my brother, for Sleepy, for my father and mother. I was doing it just so I would still be able to look the Ballplayers in the eye. I couldn't quit. If I did, I would be quitting on everybody who believed in me.

"Rosie," Coach Ski said halfway through practice, "go catch for Ryan in the bullpen."

I dragged myself over to our imaginary bullpen and squatted down. *Great. Just great.* The state championships were right around the corner, and I was spending my time at practice being ball girl.

I stood up from my catcher's position, and threw wild throws back to Ryan.

"Ugh," he said as he chased down one of my throws. He glared at me. I threw another wild one way over his head.

"Why don't you learn how to throw?"

"Fine," I said softly.

He asked for me to throw the ball, so I did just that. On my next catch, I stood up, and planted my feet. I wound up, and furiously fired the ball right back to Ryan, as if I was the pitcher and he was the catcher.

"Thank you!" Ryan said. "Finally."

What a jerk! You're just like everyone else. Nobody wants me here except Sleepy. I put all my anger and frustration into every throw. After I unleashed my circle change a few times, Ryan's eyes grew interested.

"How'd ya do that?" he asked.

"It's easy," I muttered. "You go like this." I put my hand up in the air and made an OK sign with it. "Grab it with your two middle fingers," I explained.

I then placed an invisible ball in my hand, wound up, and slowly exaggerated my follow-through to show Ryan how I maneuvered my hand placement.

"Cool," he said back, and he tried throwing one. I patiently explained it again. On his second one, he improved.

"See," I called out, "it's easy."

In the meantime, Doc had been on the mound pitching. I looked over at the two scrimmaging teams, and my eyes stopped on him.

"I'm beat," he said as he wiped his brow. "How about somebody relieving me?"

The boys in the outfield shot their hands up, and screamed and yelped as if their pants were on fire.

"Me! Me! I will! I will!"

I said nothing. I just stood off to the side slapping a ball in and out of my mitt. I looked up once and noticed that Doc had ignored all the begging chants, and was walking toward our bullpen.

"Ryan can't pitch," Coach Ski yelled to Doc. "He needs to rest that arm."

Without a word, Doc adjusted his cap and continued toward us. "How 'bout you, Rosie?" he asked as he grew closer. "Ryan's got to rest his arm for the weekend. And I've seen out of the corner of my eye that you can get it across the plate. What do ya say?"

I shrugged my shoulders and stubbornly continued to play my own game of catch with my ball and glove.

"Rosie?" Doc repeated.

I picked my head up and looked around at my jealous teammates. Then I glared over to Coach Ski, who was set in the on-deck circle. Doc grew closer to me and whispered, "Now is your chance."

His words slowly pulled my attention to him. I looked into his eyes and he winked confidently. He had something in mind. Even though I didn't know what it was, I had a good feeling. I let go of the pressure that had built up inside of me, and jogged out to the mound.

Vic was up first.

"Fan him outta there, Rosie," Cowboy hollered. "Sit him down."

I delivered the first pitch, and Vic let it pass. He practiced his swing, and looked me right in the eye. I threw a fastball, then a wild change-up right by his bat for strikes one and two.

"He couldn't have hit those with a tennis racket," Cowboy jeered.

I moved the ball slowly around in my glove. I wanted to get one good feel of it before I threw my specialty. A deep breath settled me down for a few seconds. I wound up and let the smooth hardball go.

Vic swung wildly, and missed. He grunted and then pounded his bat against the ground in frustration. As he slowly walked out of the batter's box, the guys in the field laughed and cheered.

"Have a seat, Vic-Man!" Fish shouted.

There always seemed to be a bonus round of razzing and jeering if it was a girl who made a boy look bad. I hated it when boys did that.

"Way to go, Rosie," Sleepy said calmly from his catching position. My best friend was not at all surprised by my performance.

The celebration faded fast when I looked to my right. I watched Coach Ski saunter his stocky, pigeon-toed, beer-bellied body up to the plate.

"Back it up, boys," he said arrogantly.

I looked him square in the eyes. I wanted this business over and done with as quickly as possible. I wound up and threw a fastball right down the pipe.

"Back it up even further outfield," Coach Ski said after he let it pass. His words made me recall what Mr. Martino said to me during the regular season when he tried to hit off me. *I've got to mix it up.* So I threw a wild change-up that dipped out of the strike zone. Coach Ski impatiently took a stab at it. He tipped it foul.

My next fastball was too high. He let it go past him. I spoon fed him another tantalizing change-up next, and he snapped his bat around too quickly again for his second foul ball.

"He's in trouble now," Cowboy bellowed from short.

Coach Ski's face turned red and he began to sweat as Cowboy continued to jabber.

"It's come down to one pitch," Cowboy said. "What's he gonna do?"

I ran a quick review of the pitches I had thrown. I had one huge pitch left. And as Mr. Martino always said, I needed to throw every bit of mustard I had on it.

I rested the ball in my glove. With my right hand, I reached up and flipped my cap backwards. I rolled the smooth, cool leather and the line of bumpy threads around in my hand. I closed my eyes and took a deep breath. When I opened them, I saw Sleepy nod his head. I zeroed in on Sleepy's glove, wound up, and threw the meanest circle change of my life.

Coach Ski whiffed by a mile. Everyone froze. Even Nick and Ryan stood stunned, with their mouths dropped open.

"She's done it, folks!" Cowboy finally shrieked. "She kicked the Big Man's butt right outta there."

Everyone erupted into laughter and cheers. I finally felt as if I could breathe again.

"Nice pitch, Rosie," Coach Ski said lowly as he walked off. I caught Doc out of the corner of my eye, and he gave me a thumbs-up sign. I looked to Sleepy, who was standing up and holding the ball behind home plate.

All I could see were sparkling, pearly-white teeth.

• • • •

As Sleepy's mother drove us home that night, I looked into the pink and orange sky. We still had some daylight left.

"Let's go to the park," I said.

"Can I, Mom?" Sleepy asked.

"Make sure you're home before dark," she said as she stopped the car.

Sleepy and I jumped out and raced down to the park, where we met up with the Ballplayers.

"How was practice?" Penny asked.

"It was great!" shouted Sleepy. "Rosie struck out Coach Ski."

"You did?" gasped Molly.

"You should have seen the look on his face," Sleepy went on. "Even the twins couldn't believe it. I think they wanted to celebrate a little, too."

"He stinks," I said and everyone burst out laughing. I grinned a proud smile. Sleepy ran off to hang out with Eddie and J.J. on the corner.

"That coach better play you," Wil said to me. "We're not going all the way out to your games anymore if you're on the bench. I had to hold Molly back from going up and telling the guy off."

Molly, whose temper often got the best of her, shrugged innocently. "Hey," she said with a mischievous grin. "Let's go to the Drill Sergeant's house."

The Drill Sergeant's real name was Shawn Plumley. He lived in a two-story house on the south end of the park and ran track at the local junior college. His muscles, black buzz cut, beady brown eyes, and booming voice made him a perfect fit for the army in our minds. So we nicknamed him "Drill Sergeant."

On boring summer nights, we entertained ourselves by pestering people in the neighborhood like "Drill Sergeant." We became quite skilled at snooping around. Our little games of cat and mouse tested our speed and courage, as well as the Sergeant's hot temper.

"We're gonna get caught one of these times," Penny moaned.

"Come on, P," Wil pleaded. "Stop worrying so much. He won't catch any of us."

I looked at Angel, who always needed a little extra convincing, too. She winked and smiled at me. She was in. Now that we had Angel on our side, we turned back to Penny.

"It's no big deal," Molly tried to explain.

"If you don't come with us, we're telling everyone you are in love with Cowboy," threatened Wil.

A little blackmail always did the trick. Penny knew the consequences of such a rumor. A few seconds passed before she sighed loudly and agreed to go along with us.

"No rocks," Angel said. One week earlier, a group of kids found themselves in a heap of trouble when they were caught throwing rocks.

Molly scoffed. "We're not stupid," she said.

"Use a tennis ball," Wil added.

"I'll go get one," Molly said and she took off.

"Don't throw it too hard, Rosie," pleaded Angel nervously.

Five minutes later, Molly returned. We huddled together to go over the plan.

"I don't know," said Wil nervously as if she suddenly wanted to back out.

"Come on," Molly said. Her blue eyes begged Wil to relax. "Don't be such a wimp, Wil. It's just a little fun."

"Yeah – it's no big deal," Wil mumbled. "Right. For you it isn't."

Everyone knew that Wilma Rudolph Thomas' large frame did not allow her to run anything like the track star she was named after.

"I'll hang back with you," Angel offered.

"You better not leave me," Wil said.

"I won't," Angel said. "I promise."

"I can't believe I'm doing this again," Penny muttered.

We had pestered Shawn Plumley two other times before without even coming close to getting caught. We had one close call when Wil yelled frantically from behind some bushes, "I'm gonna wet my pants", and almost blew our cover. Fortunately Molly and Penny dragged her out of the yard she was hiding in, pulled her down an alley, and through the park. There they stuffed her in a tunnel on the playground until she hushed up and gained control of herself.

"Anyone have to go?" Angel asked seriously.

We all knew who and what she was referring to.

"You better go now," Penny said to Wil, "or else we're all in trouble."

"I'm fine," Wil said coolly. "Is your arm warmed up, Rosie?"

I nodded proudly, knowing I was regarded as the best object thrower in the group. We scurried in the direction of the Plumley's house, holding our panting breaths down, and trying to swallow our giggles.

"Shhhh," Molly hushed.

Molly, Penny, and I crept into the backyard and hid behind a big oak tree. We looked back to a neighbor's shed, where we left Angel and Wil hiding. It was a safe 50 yards behind.

Molly slapped the fuzzy tennis ball in my hand. I looked up and eyed a spot on the building just beneath Shawn Plumley's bedroom window.

"Go ahead," Penny whispered. She looked back at Wil and gave her the nod to start running for cover.

I looked up at my target and could see the flickering light from the television in his room. I wound up, and the ball slipped off my fingers and sailed a bit higher than I anticipated. I held my hand up just long enough to see the ball disappear into the house. The window had no screen. I froze and winced in fear of hearing a crash.

"Come on!" Penny whispered frantically. I quickly breathed a brief sigh of relief when I heard no crashing noise, and then sprinted madly after my friends.

Just as I turned the corner, I heard the slam of the back door, which meant the Drill Sergeant was on the loose.

"I'm gonna get you rotten kids!" he screamed.

We all took different routes across the park, bolting through alleys and cutting across the sidewalks of Broadway and Woodside. I picked my speed up, turned a corner, and rolled underneath Old Man Miller's porch. I was safe there. I breathed quietly and looked out from underneath my hiding spot. My eyes turned toward a pair of glowing white legs and striped green sneakers. It was Molly.

I knew better than to shout her name. Within seconds, I heard heavy feet pound the sidewalk and held my breath. We both didn't move for two more minutes. I laid there listening to the car engines roar and watching beams from the headlights pass. When the coast was clear, I crawled out from under my hiding spot and stood up in the darkness of night.

"Molly," I called out after I looked down the street both ways, "he's gone."

She burst into laughter as she crawled out from behind the garbage cans. "You threw it right into his house! Did you see that?"

A hinge squeaked, and we both jumped.

"Phew," sighed Molly. Penny emerged from the backyard next door. She buckled over in laughter.

Wil and Angel came jogging down the street smiling and giggling.

"Let's do it again!" Wil said.

"Yeah, right," Angel said. "I almost killed myself trying to pull you out of that mess."

"Nice throw, Rosie," Molly said.

"I didn't mean to throw it right in," I said defensively. "It slipped."

"Whether you meant it or not, it was hysterical," Molly said. "Did you see how fast he came running out of there?"

No damage was done, so I relaxed. We laughed for a good 10 minutes, and each took turns telling our version of the prank, except for Penny. She just stood there shaking her head with a nervous laughter now and then. The sky turned completely dark except for the bright slice of the moon, and parents' voices started calling us in for the night.

"What were you laughing about?" Sleepy asked as he ran up alongside of me.

"You missed it," I said. "We hit the Drill Sergeant's house."

"With a rock?" Sleepy gasped in fear.

"No way," I shook my head. "With a tennis ball. I'd be grounded forever if I broke a window."

"Or you would just have to live in the library," Sleepy joked, and I laughed.

My smile faded as I thought about what I had just said. I would be in serious trouble if my parents found out what kind of stupid stuff we did for the sake of feeling wild sometimes, especially if they knew it involved my throwing anything at somebody's house.

I crept into my bed that night thinking about my awesome circle change at practice. Then I thought of my near devastating throw at the Sergeant's house. I began to wonder whether I had flirted with the invincibility complex that I had heard so much about in regards to my brother. I pushed my tattered mitt off the side of my bed, and it fell to the floor. The *coquí* charm sparkled up at me.

Maybe I had a little luck after all.

Chapter Thirteen

"**B**ring it in, guys!" Coach Ski yelled as his brow furrowed.

"Let's go!" Doc cheered.

The eager, buzzing crowd arrived early to catch every second of the action for our first weekend of state championship baseball. A group of feisty, red-clad fans had traveled down with our opponent, the Bridgeview Redbirds. The Redbirds always made a strong showing during the championship season.

Coach Ski called out our positions as we bustled around the dugout. I eagerly awaited my assignment. When the list ended without my name being called, my heart sank. The last glimmer of hope I had for playing faded out of my sight.

All of the starters rushed excitedly onto the field except Cowboy. Taking his time, he finished gulping down his last mouthful of water, tossed the paper cup in the garbage can, and stood up. Then he took one deep breath.

"You all right, Cowboy?" I asked quietly.

He said nothing as he strutted out of the dugout. He stopped next to Coach Ski. "Coach," Cowboy said softly.

Coach Ski didn't hear him. "Coach Ski!" he said louder.

Coach Ski finally turned over his shoulder and stared down at him.

"What's the matter, Cowboy?" he asked. "Why aren't you on the field?"

"I'm not playing, Coach," Cowboy said evenly.

Coach Ski bent over, grabbed his knees, and looked Cowboy in the eye.

"Why?" Coach Ski asked.

Cowboy stared at the ground.

"You sick?" Coach Ski asked.

Cowboy shook his head.

"You hurt?"

Cowboy's gentle brown eyes gazed up and off in the distance. He shook his head again.

"What's the matter, then?"

"Somebody else deserves to be playing," Cowboy mumbled.

"What?" Coach Ski asked in disbelief.

"I don't want to make you mad," Cowboy began, "but if I were playing better than a lot of kids and nobody gave me a chance, I would have quit a long time ago."

A lump formed in my throat. I hid my wide eyes under the bill of my cap. *What is he doing?* My mind raced in fear for Cowboy. He was in deep trouble now. I held my breath waiting for Coach Ski to launch into a tirade.

But that was the end of the conversation. I watched Cowboy's big feet walk past me and sit down on the bench. An awkward moment of silence passed.

"Rosie," Coach Ski called out, "take short."

I picked my head up and turned toward Cowboy. I didn't know what to say or do.

"Go ahead," he said quietly as he stared straight ahead. "You had better hurry up."

"Let's go, Rosie!" Coach Ski hollered.

I jumped up and darted out of the dugout before Coach Ski could change his mind. I took the field and warmed up with my team as if nothing out of the ordinary had just taken place.

Before the first pitch, I couldn't help but turn my eyes to the dugout. Cowboy picked up his head and gave me a confident nod. I smiled as I squatted into my ready position. I finally had my chance.

For the first time as an all-star, I didn't worry about being benched. I just played. I stopped every ball that went my way. I had to. I owed it to Cowboy.

After I stopped one ball, I heard my dad yell, "Way to go, kid!" I couldn't believe my ears. I looked up and my father was smiling. He was beaming. He was so happy and so excited, he kept adjusting and re-adjusting his hat on his head as he paced behind the backstop.

I turned my attention back to the field. Most of the Redbird's hits landed in center, and Vic was having a tough time keeping the hits in front of him.

"Come on, Vic!" Coach Ski screamed. "Get your head in the game and start playing!"

I wondered what Coach Ski was like when he was my age. Maybe none of the kids in his neighborhood ever let him play. Maybe that's why he was so miserable.

It was the bottom of the fifth. Ryan stepped up to plate and belted a double. I followed him up to bat.

"Let's go, kid!" my dad screamed.

My nerves tingled and my palms began to sweat. I had already struck out once that day after trying to nail the ball out of the park. I couldn't screw up again. If I did, my father wouldn't remember any of my good plays. He would only remind me of the bad ones.

"Rosie," Doc said. "Come here."

I jogged down the sideline and stopped in front of him. He bent over to look me in the eye.

"Just connect, Rosie," Doc said. "That's what makes you a good hitter. You're consistent. Knock us around the bases, and let the power hitters do their job."

I nodded my head, and trotted into the box. *Just like Roberto Clemente.* I released a graceful, quick swing, and connected solidly for a single over the second baseman's head. My hit advanced Ryan to third.

Our fans clapped and cheered for me.

"Atta girl!" Doc hollered excitedly.

I didn't look at my father. I was tired of checking in with him on every play. He wanted me to be perfect. I couldn't be perfect. I was just happy to be playing – nothing else mattered.

I kept my eyes on Doc, whose hands were busy communicating with me. He gave me the steal sign as I expected. The pitcher wound up and threw a wild throw that went high over the catcher's head. Ryan darted for home, and slid safely. I rounded second and broke for third, hoping the pitcher and catcher would have forgotten about me. When the crowd roared, the catcher turned and rifled the ball down the baseline. I picked up my speed and hit the dirt. I beat the throw by a mile.

"She's a thief!" joked Vic as our fans cheered.

I grinned, brushing myself off, and I caught my breath. It felt good to know that I had lifted my team's spirits. At the inning's end, we had pulled ourselves up by two runs.

Before taking the field for defense, Doc called me over. "Rosie," he said calmly. "Cowboy's back at short, and we're moving you out to center. Keep playing tough. Don't let anything get by."

I nodded my head, and smiled as Cowboy passed me. "Let's do this, now," Cowboy cheered. "Put a stop to 'em."

I stayed at center field for the rest of the game, where I caught one fly ball, and made two stops to help us win the first game 6-3.

In the second game, with one inning left, we were up 8-2. I watched Coach Ski and Doc huddle together in a private discussion before we went up to bat. Coach Ski nodded his head, and Doc called out my name.

"Rosie," Doc said to me. "Warm up your arm."

I turned to Sleepy and his eyebrows raised. As we walked outside the fence, I looked over at Rico. He winked, and I grinned.

After a couple of throws, Sleepy stood up and walked toward me. "You're ready," he said.

I jogged onto the field with an easy smile. It was as if I knew all along that everything was going to work out the way it did that afternoon.

"One, two, three, kid," Doc called as I took the mound. "Show 'em what you got."

I struck out the first two batters, which shocked the majority of the fans and opposing players. My teammates laughed at the expressions on the Redbird's faces.

"He's no hitter!" Luke cheered. "Sit 'em down, Rosie."

"One more, Rosa!" my mother cheered excitedly from behind the fence. The third batter dribbled a ball to Cowboy at short, and he threw the runner out with ease.

"There's your perfect inning," Cowboy said as we ran in together.

"Thanks, Cowboy," I said softly.

I had never seen a person my age stand up for anyone the way he did for me that day. Cowboy looked at me, but he let my words pass without taking any credit.

"One weekend down, and two to go!" he hollered.

We both joined the rest of our team to celebrate.

Chapter Fourteen

The second I heard the crack of the bat, I knew the action was coming my way. I sprinted to my right, stuck out my glove, and lunged to the ball. But it fell out of my reach. I quickly scooped it up and fired the ball to my relay man, who passed it back to Ryan on the pitcher's mound. Then I heard my father scream.

"You're not ready out there!" he yelled. "Wake up!"

I waited for Coach Ski to blast me for not making the catch.

"Shake it off, Rosie!" Coach Ski yelled enthusiastically. "You'll get the next one!"

My eyes grew wide. I could not believe my ears. Then I looked at the scoreboard. That explained why Coach Ski was so calm. With two innings left in the second game of the semi-finals, we were coasting on an 8-3 lead.

Later in the dugout, I turned to Sleepy, who had spent most of the afternoon behind the plate. Streaks of dirt and sweat ran down his face.

"You okay, Sleep?" I asked.

When Sleepy barely nodded his head, Doc stepped in the dugout and hollered, "Anyone want to catch and give Sleepy a rest?" He glanced around at our sweaty, tired faces. Nobody moved.

"I will," I said.

"Suit up, Rosie," Doc ordered.

When the inning ended, I quickly fastened the buckles on my chest protector and chin guards. I crouched behind the plate, and held my mitt up to provide a big target.

Cowboy was chanting, "Ry-Ski, Ry-Ski, Ry-Ski!"

Ryan threw two fastballs. Each one stung my hand all the way down to the bone. I swallowed the pain, and tossed the ball back effortlessly.

With one out left in the game and a runner on first, we were on the verge of wrapping the game up for the day.

"Throw my specialty," I called out to Ryan. Ryan pressed his lips together and smiled as he wound up for the circle change. The ball zoomed towards me riding down and then whipping out to the right. It was perfect. I was so busy watching the pitch that I almost missed the catch completely. At the last second, I reached out and knocked it down. I spun around looking for the loose ball. But I couldn't find it. Everyone was screaming, "Get it, get it!" even though I didn't know where to look. I glanced to the infield and my worried eyes followed the runner as he was heading to third. I threw off my helmet, spun around and then ran to the backstop, thinking that maybe the ball got caught in a rut by the fence.

I found nothing. The ball had disappeared. The crowd continued to scream, and so did my teammates. I kept running around in circles.

The runner crossed home plate safely, and the opposing fans went wild in cheers and laughter. Ryan came running in to the plate with his eyes wide and pointing at me. He took a deep breath and his shoulders dropped. Then he pointed his finger closer to my chest protector.

"It's in there," he quipped, and he reached no further.

I dropped my head down, and my face burned in embarrassment. I pulled the ball out, and everyone in the ballpark exploded in laughter. My popping eyes looked up at Ryan, and his intense look broke into a forgiving smile. If the score were any closer, the coaches, players and fans wouldn't have thought it was so funny. But with one out left, the chance to play in the state finals belonged to us.

"Way to play, kids!" Luke's mother said after the game. She then looked at me and smiled. "Did you lose something out there, Rosie?" she joked.

"Nice job, Rosie Jonzie!" Mr. Martino bellowed. He gently knocked my cap down onto my nose. "You and Sleep are doing great! One weekend left to bring the championship to the city. Go get 'em!"

Mr. Baker walked up to me and tapped me on the cap. "Way to play!" he said. "I knew you could do it. You're determined — just like your brother."

I smiled and thanked Mr. Baker.

"Stop by the cages this week," he said as he walked away. "You've gotta be ready for the championship!"

I turned and looked up at a stranger who was carrying a red notebook. He had a bushy mustache, beady eyes, and a pencil resting on his ear.

"I'm Fred Jefferson with the *Herald-Journal*," he said to me with a smile. "That was a great game you played today."

I peered up at him suspiciously. I recalled the lousy things the newspaper reported when Rico chose to give the pros a shot instead of going to college. Then I thought of how I read in my book that Roberto Clemente never trusted the media. I looked away from the man and kept quiet.

"I was thinking of writing a little story on you," he added.

After working so hard to escape the spotlight, I wanted no part of a reporter or any newspaper.

"Do you mind if I ask you some questions?" he insisted.

I looked over to my celebrating teammates over at the concession stand. I wanted to be with them, so I turned and walked away. Then I felt a hand grab my shoulder. It was my father. He steered me right back into the conversation.

"I'm James Jones, Rosalinda's father," my dad interrupted with a smile as he extended his hand to the strange man. "Rosie's been playing ever since she was two..."

My father told my life story, and the reporter diligently scribbled everything down. He asked me a few questions, and I purposely gave him only "yes" and "no" answers. I figured that anything more would have made me sound cocky. The only full sentence I said was, "All of us just want to win."

Once I received permission from my father to leave the boring conversation, I darted over to the concession stand.

"Can I have your autograph?" Vic asked.

"When you're famous," Cowboy added with a grin, "don't forget us little people."

I tried to hide my smile under my cap.

• • • •

My mother's loud voice woke me up the next morning. She was talking on the telephone.

"Doesn't she look beautiful!" she raved and then paused. "It's such a great picture, and a wonderful story," she added.

I trudged out of bed and reached the kitchen just as she hung up the phone.

"Look," she said.

My eyes zeroed in on the photo of my catching a fly ball during warm-ups. I sat down at the kitchen and read the story. I was surprised to read the nice things Coach Ski said about me, but I groaned when I saw my father's embarrassing quotes about my growing up. Then I sighed when I read what the reporter wrote about the ball getting caught in my chest protector.

"What's the matter, Rosa?" my mother asked.

"Nothing," I moaned.

"You should be proud of yourself!" she said.

I heard the front door slam. My father walked into the kitchen. He bent down and put his arm around me. "You played a great game last night," he said.

I didn't know whether or not to believe him. I'm sure my picture being in the Sunday paper made him feel good. Maybe he was beginning to feel bad about the way he had been treating me.

"We are so proud of you," my mother said. She wrapped her arms around me after my father let go. I winced as she pressed her painted lips against my cheek. She then disappeared into the living room.

Rico walked into the kitchen with his shirt unbuttoned and his hair still wet from the shower. I could smell his heavy cologne as he sat down at the table.

"Good morning, Champ," he said.

"I read one of my books about Roberto last night," I said. I started telling my brother all about Roberto's batting titles and the world championship teams he won.

"He must have been so good," I said in awe.

"Roberto was one of the best, all right," Rico replied, and his voice trailed off.

"Have you heard from your agent?" I whispered.

He nodded and looked into the other room to make sure no one heard what I had said. "He said he'll be letting me know soon," he said quietly.

"When?" I asked.

"This week," he added. He picked up the paper and smiled at my picture. "He promised by Tuesday or Wednesday."

"When would you leave?" I anxiously asked.

"I don't know," he added. "Probably as soon as I can."

My smile faded. It hurt to think of my brother not being around anymore.

Chapter Fifteen

I called up Sleepy on Tuesday morning.

"You wanna go to the library?" I asked. "Rico said he'd drop us off."

"Sure," Sleepy said. "I'll be right over."

"Don't say anything to Rico about his agent and baseball," I whispered into the phone. "He hasn't heard anything yet. He should find out this week."

"Okay," Sleepy agreed.

A few minutes later, Sleepy was at my front door. We ran outside and tossed the ball around as we waited for Rico.

"You two ready?" Rico asked as he pushed open the front door.

"We're always ready, Ric," Sleepy said confidently.

My brother grinned. "It seems like you two *like* going to the library," he said as we walked over to the car.

I shrugged my shoulders. I didn't want him to think I was turning into a nerd. And I also didn't want word to get back to my parents that they had gotten the best of me with their punishment.

"It's all right," I mumbled.

Rico dropped us off in front of the library.

"Have fun," he said, "and stay out of trouble."

Sleepy and I ran up the stairs and pushed open the heavy library door. I slowed down when I stepped inside. My eyes were stuck to the red construction paper on the bulletin board behind the main desk. It had my newspaper article and photo pinned to it.

"What a wonderful story!" Ms. Daniel exclaimed when she saw me. "No wonder why you love to read those baseball books so much, Rosie."

My face felt hot. I didn't want everyone to think I really wanted my picture up there. I thought about asking her if I could take it down, but I knew that would hurt her feelings. She wouldn't understand all that I had been through.

"When is your next game?" Ms. Daniel asked.

"Saturday at Twin Park," Sleepy said. "It's for the state championship."

"Great!" she said excitedly. "Maybe I will go and watch."

I smiled a thank-you and we went to our table. Sleepy and I spent some time drawing silly pictures of people on scrap paper.

"We better start reading," Sleepy said after he grew tired of our goofy drawings.

I did my best to get through my book on Roberto, and Sleepy did the same for his book on Jackie Robinson. With about 15 minutes left in our visit, I started talking again. But this time, it was about something important.

"Sleepy," I said. "If you tell me about Jackie, I'll tell you about Roberto."

"Okay," Sleepy said after he cleared his throat. "Jackie Robinson loved all sports. He played basketball, baseball, football, and track and field at UCLA. He was the first African-American to play in the major leagues. He played with the Brooklyn Dodgers."

"Shhh," Ms. Daniel hushed from behind her desk.

"We're talking about our books," Sleepy explained.

"You are?" Ms. Daniel replied.

"Yeah," Sleepy said. "I'm telling Rosie about Jackie Robinson and she's going to tell me all about Roberto Clemente."

"That's a great idea," Ms. Daniel said. "Sounds just like an oral book report."

I cringed at the thought of doing a book report in the summer.

"When you're done with your book reports, you should write a few paragraphs about each other, and then you can read them to me."

"Yeah," Sleepy said.

I didn't think it was a bad idea either. I loved to write about other people, especially good people like Sleepy.

"Finish what you're doing," Ms. Daniel said. "I'm sorry for interrupting."

My eyes turned back to Sleepy. "Jackie Robinson won player of the year once and he got into the Hall of Fame in..." he looked up to the ceiling deep in thought. "It was 1962."

"Wow," I said. "You remembered a lot, Sleep."

"Tell me about Roberto," he asked.

"Roberto was born in Puerto Rico. He played baseball so much that his mother used to have to remind him to eat. He first played with the Brooklyn Dodgers. Then he ended up with the Pittsburgh Pirates. He helped them win the World Series. Three times, I think. And he won the batting title one year. Roberto fought for equal rights for all baseball players."

"Kind of like Jackie," Sleepy said.

"Yeah," I replied. "He even won the Most Valuable Player award one year. The sad part is that Roberto died in a plane crash. There was an earthquake and he wanted to get people food. His plane crashed."

Sleepy's eyes turned sad, and so did mine.

"Are you finished?" Ms. Daniel called out.

We nodded eagerly. She came over to the table, and set down fresh sheets of paper and markers.

"I can't wait to read what you have to write," she said.

About 10 minutes later, Sleepy and I were both finished. We told Ms. Daniel, and she pulled a chair up to our table.

"You begin first, Rosie," she said.

I started to read what I had written on my paper.

Sleepy

Sleepy Jackson lives next door to me. His real name is Scotty, but we all call him Sleepy because he looks kind of tired.

He's really a nice person, and always likes to smile. He's a great baseball player, too. He hits a lot of home runs and my brother Rico has to buy him a milkshake for every one.

One day when something was bugging me, Sleepy made me feel better. I wanted to quit the team we're on, but Sleepy wouldn't let me. I feel better now because I didn't.

Sleepy is also very smart. He really likes coming to the library. I have one more thing to write about Sleepy that I am very proud of: He's my best friend.

"Very nice, Rosie," Ms. Daniel said. Sleepy blushed. Then he cleared his throat and began to read the words on his paper.

> ### Rosie Jones
>
> My friend Rosie is a great friend and a great, great baseball player. We play baseball every day almost all day except when we're in the library. She's good at everything. She can hit, catch, throw, and steal bases like a thief.
>
> Sometimes people don't think she's going to be good enough for them beadse she's a girl. But she always shows them and then they change their minds. I'm glad Rosie is on my team with me. It wouldn't be any fun without her.

I smiled proudly.

"That's so nice of you," Ms. Daniel said. "You both write very well."

Being at the library was a lot of fun that day. I rushed into the house later that afternoon to check and see if Rico had heard anything. I couldn't find him. I picked up a note on the table. It read:

> Rosie,
> I went to the cages.
> Mama will be home at 4:30.
> P.S. I haven't heard anything yet.
> Rico

My mother walked through the front door just as I crumpled up the note. Then the phone rang. I raced to it hoping that it would be the big call for Rico, but it was my Aunt Clara.

Every night that week, I jumped to the phone, but the call never came.

By Friday, Rico didn't even bother to come home.

Chapter Sixteen

On Saturday morning I sat dressed in my uniform on our front porch. I tossed the ball in and out of my mitt as I waited for my parents. When I heard the purr of Rico's Mustang, my heart skipped a beat.

"Hi," I said as he slammed the car door shut. I looked carefully to check his spirits. His eyes looked sad, but when he looked at me, he grinned.

"Are you excited?" he asked.

I smiled as he slowly walked up to me, and draped his arm over my shoulder. "Hammer away today, kid," he said.

I looked into his weary eyes. I didn't know what I could possibly say to make him feel better. I wanted to tell him not to worry and that everything would be OK. But I knew he had told himself that many times before.

"Hit one for me," he said.

I nodded my head and said, "I will."

At the ballpark, we ran through warm-ups without much conversation. The crowd grew larger by the minute. My dad started pacing and fidgeting more than ever before. I looked over my shoulder and saw the Ballplayers huddled together outside the fence.

"Yeah, Rosie!" Wil yelled.

I waved my mitt and grinned as I ran into the dugout. My eyes stopped on Cowboy as he turned over pieces of equipment. "Where did you leave it last, Nick?" he asked.

"I don't know," Nick whined and his eyes shifted about nervously.

"What are you looking for?" I asked.

"His batting glove," Cowboy replied.

My heart sank. We were five minutes away from the start of the state championship series, and our star second baseman and back-up pitcher was without his lucky batting glove.

"I think I brought it in here and left it on the cooler," Nick said. "Maybe it fell into the garbage can."

Cowboy bent over and stuck his head in the deep garbage can and poked through it with his mitt. "Yuk!" he moaned. "You don't need it anyway, Nick. You hit a great shot that day in practice when I borrowed it from you. You can do it again."

"I need it," Nick implored. "I gotta have it."

"It's okay," I said softly. "We need you, Nick."

Nick grimaced as the rest of the team poured into the dugout.

"Fire up, guys!" Doc cheered.

I was the lead-off batter. I looked to check Nick's condition before I walked up to the plate. His eyes watered as he kept moving things around in the dugout.

The crowd roared when I stepped up to the plate, and then again when I hit the ball down the third base line for a single. Luke batted second, and he also connected for a single. I stole third on a wild pitch while Joe was at the plate. My eyes caught Nick in the on-deck circle. He had his cap and helmet pulled down over his somber eyes.

On the next pitch, Joe flied out. Nick stepped up and whiffed hard on two pitches in a row.

"Connect, Nick!" Coach Ski shouted.

Nick took a ball then missed again on the next. My nerves tightened as he walked back to the dugout. I could tell by Nick's stubborn scowl that he was convinced he couldn't hit without his batting glove.

"What are you doing?" Ryan asked loudly as Nick walked past him.

"Shut up!" Nick shot back.

That was just the beginning. Slowly our team began to crumble. Each of us took turns striking out and making mental mistakes. We lost our first game 3-0 after playing our worst baseball of the season.

"What's the matter with you guys?" Coach Ski shouted before the second game. No one responded. "You're so slow in the field. Everyone is taking their eye off the ball. What's the deal? This is it, guys. These are the big ones. Let's put everything else behind us and go after it!"

We trudged through the first three innings of the second game. Ryan, who had been keeping us in the game with his forceful pitching arm, stepped up to the plate and smashed a hard grounder to the outfield. He rounded first and followed his father's shouts to go for two. The right fielder gunned the ball to the second baseman, who had crouched down for the catch and tag. We screamed, "Down!" and Ryan launched his body down for the slide.

The two bodies tangled, and I saw Ryan's ankle twist in an awkward position. Then he shrieked in pain. His father sprinted out to him, while the rest of us held our breaths in the dugout.

A crowd of coaches and umpires gathered around the base. When Ryan stopped crying, we all relaxed. Then the crowd started to murmur. Everyone knew that an injury to one of the best players in the state could have a devastating effect on our chances for victory.

After about five minutes, Coach Ski emerged from the huddle with Ryan cradled in his arms. We cleared a spot for him on the bench and his father gently set him down.

"Nick," Coach Ski said. "Warm up."

Nick stood looking stunned. He could not believe how much pain his brother was in. He remained frozen.

"Let's go," Coach said firmly. "You gotta get that arm loose."

Without any sign of confidence, Nick dragged himself out to the bullpen. *Come on, Nick! Three more innings. That's all.*

Nick kicked a few stones and stirred up the dirt.

"You can do it!" Coach Ski hollered. It seemed as if he suddenly realized that Nick had the jitters. "Right down the pipe. You got a tough defense behind you, so don't worry."

The crowd buzzed with anticipation. But all the cheers in the world couldn't have snapped Nick out of his fearful trance. His arm looked tight, and his pitches went wild. After he walked three batters in a row, everyone on our side gasped.

"Time-out please!" Cowboy screamed from shortstop.

"What?" Coach Ski exclaimed on the sideline.

"Everybody in!" Cowboy yelled. We all rushed into the pitcher's mound. Coach Ski fumed as he marched his way out of the dugout. His eyes were locked on Cowboy.

"Hang on," I heard Doc say to Coach Ski as I ran in from left field. "Give them a second."

"What is that kid doing?" Coach Ski asked.

"Let them go," Doc said. "We still have another time-out left." Coach Ski stopped just short of stepping on the field. He looked up at the scoreboard. It read: Indians 3 Sluggers 2.

I put my attention in our team huddle. All eyes turned to Cowboy. "We can't give up any more runs," he said. "We need you, Nick. Everyone needs each other."

"You can do it, Nick," I added.

We shouted "Win!" and ran back on to the field. While the rest of the team jogged off, Cowboy stayed behind.

"You've always said that glove is the only way we could tell you two apart," he said.

I slowed down and listened carefully.

"We know who you are," Cowboy said. "Show everybody else right now."

Nick picked his eyes up off the ball in his glove and he looked at Cowboy. He then turned to the dugout, where his brother sat with his ankle propped up and wrapped in ice. His father was sitting on the bench next to Ryan. Nick slapped the ball hard in his mitt and took the mound.

After he hurled a series of perfect fastballs, Nick stood taller on the mound. We cheered wildly. He pulled us out of the inning alive and then got us off to a good start at the plate by socking a double into right field.

"Way to go, Nick!" hollered Ryan, who had pulled himself up the metal fence, and was standing on one foot. Doc grabbed him on the shoulder and made him sit back down.

● ● ● ●

We won our second game, which tied the series at 1-1. During the sixth inning of our last game, we pulled ahead 2-1 after Sleepy blasted a shot deep into left. The tug-of-war continued without any change in momentum or either team scoring. It came down to the end. With two runners on, we needed one last out. Then the state championship would be ours.

All the fans in the ballpark were on their feet. My mother peeked from under her hands. I heard her scream "Hammer away!" I rolled my eyes because we were in the outfield. Then I took one look down at my sparkling *coquí* charm, and hoped that we could hold on for one more out.

Nick pulled the ball close to his chest, bent his left knee up, kicked it out, and delivered the pitch right down the pipe. The ball jumped off the bat and sailed right in my direction.

I took a simple two steps in, reached up, and plucked the ball out of the sky for the easy catch. Everyone leapt into the air. I ran to Nick at the mound, and joined the infielders, who had already fallen into a pile.

"You did it, Nick-Ski!" Cowboy shouted from the bottom. "That's my boy!"

Fish and Joe, who were in the dugout, slung Ryan's arms over their shoulders and slowly walked him out to the celebration on the field.

"Yeah, yeah, yeah!" Ryan exclaimed, and he gave his brother a high five.

Our pack streamed from the mound into the dugout as the crowd gave us a standing ovation. Then my eyes caught Cowboy carefully reaching into his pocket. He pulled out a batting glove – Nick's batting glove.

"Hey Nick," Cowboy said. "See what I found."

Nick's eyes brightened. He snatched the glove away from his grinning teammate.

"Where was it?" Nick asked.

"It was under the cooler," Cowboy replied.

Instead of putting it on, Nick reached around his body and stuffed it into his back pocket. While everyone else went back to celebrating, I eyed Cowboy suspiciously. He felt the weight of my stare.

"I found it halfway through the second game," he whispered. "Don't tell him, though. He really didn't need it anyway."

I smiled at Cowboy and then I turned to my teammates. Vic whipped his cap around in the air. Sleepy jumped up on the bench, and Fish leapt up to give him a high five. After Luke dumped a jug of water all over Joe, he came running toward me. As the water dripped down my face, I laughed so hard that my sides started to ache. I settled down and looked up again at what was happening.

We had done it. We were state champions.

Chapter Seventeen

We quietly settled down in the dugout for the awards ceremony. One by one, the president of our league called us out onto the field.

I watched Joe and Luke jog out smiling. Vic pumped his fist in the air. After receiving their individual trophies, they moved down the line high-fiving each other.

Then Cowboy strutted out, grinning as he soaked in the cheers. I clapped for him, and rattled the fence of the dugout with everyone else. When the president called out Ryan's name, Nick and Joe slung Ryan's arms over their shoulders and walked him out on to the field. The crowd applauded wildly. Ryan stood with one leg bent off the ground, and leaned on his brother for balance. I had never seen the two of them so happy together.

"And last, but certainly not least," the president called out at the end of his list, "Rosalinda Jones."

I hid my eyes under my cap and I humbly walked out to join my teammates.

"Rosie...Rosie...Rosie!" Cowboy cheered as I shuffled down the line to pick up my trophy.

I picked my head up and smiled bashfully. Then I stole a glance behind the dugout. I saw my mother snapping her camera, and my father's glowing face.

My eyes stopped on Rico. He winked and grinned. I lifted my hat off my head and flipped it backwards.

When I heard Coach Ski's name called, I watched him saunter up to the portable table of trophies, and shake hands with the president. His smug grin grew when the president placed the trophy in his hands. I breathed a deep sigh of relief. My days of dealing with him were over. I began to wonder how I ever made it through.

There was one more award to give–the most valuable player. Cowboy started to chant Nick's name. Vic and Luke joined in.

"The most valuable player of the state championship is..." the president announced.

The two coaches and president huddled together as the crowd murmured restlessly.

"We've decided that there isn't just one most valuable player. There are twelve. Everyone on the Sluggers will get a MVP trophy for their championship effort."

We cheered triumphantly. I stopped for a second and looked at Coach Ski, and wondered why he did it. *Did he really think Ryan deserved it even though he got hurt? Did he not give it to Ryan because we were all cheering for Nick? Or did he really believe that every one of us deserved the title of most valuable player?*

No one would ever know, and in the end, it never really mattered. Our parents waited eagerly for us as we stepped outside the fence. Rico bent over and gave me a hug.

"You're all right, kid," he said softly.

My mother wrapped her arms around me and then drew me in to plant a kiss on my cheek. "I'm so proud of you, Rosie. I knew you were strong. You just had to see for yourself."

I looked at her and smiled. "Thanks, Mama," I said.

Mrs. Jackson and Ronnie joined our huddle. We joked and laughed as the other parents joined in.

"Rico," Sleepy asked as he tugged on my brother's arm. "Can I get my milkshakes now?"

"All nine of them?" Rico asked in disbelief.

"All ten, you mean," Sleepy said and then he looked around. "Who wants a milkshake?"

After some negotiating, Rico agreed upon treating every player to a soft ice cream cone.

I felt a hand tap me on the shoulder. I turned and it was Penny.

"Nice game, Rosie," she said smiling. "State champs!" she said in awe.

"You were all right," Wil said. "I could have done it. Stealing bases like you. Hitting those fastballs. Making those catches. Maybe I should be playing baseball."

"Yeah, right, Wil," Molly groaned.

Cowboy strolled our way, and Penny looked at him.

"Hi," he said softly as he looked at her. Then he joined up with the rest of the players, who were fighting for their spots in line for ice cream.

"Ohhh," Wil's eyes grew wide after Cowboy passed. "Did you see that?"

"He was giving you the eye, P," Angel teased.

"Stop," Penny said. She rolled her eyes and we all giggled.

My dad came up and rested his hand on my shoulder.

"Hi, girls," he said. "One championship down, one to go, right?"

As usual, my father could never handle one victory at a time. He was already thinking about our chances at winning our summer basketball league.

Mr. Martino came walking up with Clarissa on his hip.

"I knew you could do it!" he said, and he gave me a hug with his free hand.

"Clarissa, can you wave to Rosie?" he said. "And maybe blow her a kiss?"

She placed her hands over her round hazel eyes and curled up against her father's shoulder.

"Come on, 'Rissa," Mr. Martino pleaded. "You're going to grow up to be just like Rosie."

Clarissa lifted her chubby cheeks off her father's shoulder. She picked up her tiny hand and waved at me. Then she slapped her lips awkwardly and blew me a kiss. I giggled and waved back.

"That's my girl," Mr. Martino added proudly.

Ms. Daniel came up to me and gave me a big hug.

"You were wonderful!" she said, and I smiled.

I heard someone shout, "Little Jonzie! Little Jonzie!" I looked up and saw Mr. Baker smiling. "Way to go, kid!"

I smiled. It was one of those days that I didn't want to end. Everyone I wanted to be there was present. The crowd stayed at the concession stand, talking and eating for a long time. Coach Ski walked up to me with a smile.

"You did all right Rosie," he said, and he patted me on the head. As he walked away, I glanced up at Rico. He raised his eyebrows, shrugged and then grinned. I shook my head unable to understand Coach Ski.

Doc came up next. He bent over and put his arm around me. "You hung in there, Rosie," he said sincerely, "just like I knew you would."

I looked down at the ground. *If he only knew.*

"You're the MVP in my book," he added. He winked as he walked away.

We all talked and laughed for a long time. As the light in the sky grew dim, people started heading to the parking lot.

"Ready to go?" my dad said.

"Can I stay for a while longer?" I asked. "Just a few more minutes?"

"I'll take her," Rico offered.

"All right," my father said. "We'll see you when you get home then."

I thought it had been a perfect day, until what happened that night.

Chapter Eighteen

As Rico drove up Broadway Ave., I watched all the kids playing at Anderson Park. After all my long weekends of playing on the all-star team, I missed the kids from the neighborhood. I ran into the house when we got home.

"Can I go down to the park?" I asked my father.

"No," he said. "Your mother's got supper ready for us."

After I collapsed on the couch in my filthy uniform, I peeked to see if my mother could see me from the kitchen. Rico sat down next to me and we watched a baseball game on television together.

"You staying for dinner, Rico?" I asked.

"Yeah," he sighed. "I guess."

His eyes stared blankly at the television.

"You all right, Rico?" I said.

"Yeah," he mumbled. "I'm fine, kid. Just tired."

After such a fun day, I suddenly felt sad. I couldn't be happy for myself knowing the disappointment that my brother was going through.

"Dinner's ready," my mother called. I didn't think I could move. My body felt too comfortable to be dragged into the kitchen. I exaggerated a sigh.

"Come on, kid," Rico said. I reached my arm out to his and he pulled me up off the couch.

"Is something wrong, Rico?" my mother asked as she set down a dish on the kitchen table.

"No," Rico said, and he shrugged his shoulders.

As my father pulled in his chair, he took a deep breath. "It was so much fun watching you kids play today," he said.

I looked up at my father and was surprised by the sincerity in his voice.

"I'm so proud of you, Rosie," he added softly.

For the first time in my life, I didn't care how long his pride would last. I just smiled as I saw how happy I had made my family.

The ring of the phone snapped my attention away from my father. I jumped up and raced to it.

"Hello," I said.

"Good evening," a man's voice said. "Is Rico home?"

"Yes," I said. "May I ask who is calling?"

"His agent," he replied.

The butterflies fluttered in my stomach. My wide eyes looked at my brother, who could tell by the speechless expression on my face that it was something important. I stuck the phone toward him. He stood up and pushed his chair away from the table. I handed Rico the phone and did not leave his side.

"Hello," Rico spoke into the receiver. "Fine, how are you?"

Then there was a long pause.

"I'll be there," Rico said finally. "Thanks. I'll call you tomorrow night."

By this time, my mother and father had sensed something big was happening, too. When Rico hung up the phone, I tugged on his arm, and begged him to tell me what was happening.

"I'm leaving tomorrow," he said and he looked across the room at my parents.

"Where are you going?" my mother asked.

"To camp," he said.

The room fell silent.

"It's Triple A," Rico continued, "but my agent said there's a chance I could move up pretty fast."

My father's eyes turned glassy as he took his napkin and wiped his mouth. He cleared his throat and said, "Do you have a place to stay?"

"Yeah," Rico replied.

"What about money?" my father asked.

"I have enough," Rico said.

"I've got a little saved if you need it," my dad said.

"No, thanks," Rico said kindly. "I'm all right. It's all been arranged already. I just didn't think I was ever going to hear."

I looked up at my brother as his voice faded. For the first time in my life, I saw his eyes water.

Chapter Nineteen

Early the next morning, I rolled over in my bed and opened my eyes. I watched Rico's green duffel bag slide past my doorway. I dragged myself out of bed and walked into the bathroom. I stood in my black, pin-striped night shirt and looked at myself in the mirror. I tried running a brush through my tangled hair, but it was too painful. I returned to my room and took my Sluggers baseball cap off the back of the door. I flipped it backwards and pulled it over my head.

I then grabbed my mitt off the living room couch, and picked up a ball from the floor. The door creaked open, and I hopped down the porch stairs. I slapped the ball in and out of my mitt as I sat on the bottom step watching my brother pack his bags into his car.

"Hey, kid," he said as he walked back up to the porch. "You didn't have to get out of bed. I would have come in and said good-bye before I left."

As Rico grabbed another bag off the porch and lugged it to his car, I kept my eyes on my mitt. My coqui charm glittered in the morning sun. I smiled, thinking of all my worries and doubts with the all-star team. Then I looked at my brother and realized that he understood because he had gone through what I did so many times before. Now he would be starting something new. I wanted so badly for him to get what he wanted.

I had to give him something before he left. I looked into Rico's opened equipment bag and reached in for his glove. When I felt the cool, smooth leather in my hand, I quickly glanced up at my brother to make sure he didn't see me. I slipped the mitt out, set it on the step next to me, and then sat on it. I began untying the strand that held my *coquí* charm. When I heard footsteps behind me, my fingers froze.

The front door creaked open. My mother bent down to give me a kiss, and said, "Good morning, Rosa."

My father followed right behind her. His face was still beet red from the day before. I noticed the lines under his tired eyes.

"Do you have everything?" he called out to Rico.

My mother and father both descended the stairs, and walked closer to my brother. I went back to work. My fingers picked at the leather and I finally loosened the knot. When the charm fell into my hand, I pulled my brother's glove out from under me. I triple knotted the *coquí* charm to one of the loose strands, and then pulled it tight with my teeth.

"Come say good-bye to Rico," my mother said as she waved me over.

I tucked Rico's mitt behind my back as I walked toward him. He reached out his arm, patted me softly on the head, and then pulled me close to him.

"I'm gonna miss you, kid," he whispered. "I really am."

I wrapped my arms around his waist not wanting to let go. I hoped and prayed that everything would work out. After I finally released him, I held out his glove. He took it from me and his eyes caught the sparkle of my charm. When he grinned and winked,

161

my eyes began to water. I looked far in the distance and promised myself that I would not cry.

"I've gotta get going," Rico mumbled.

My mother sniffled as she wrapped her arms around Rico. Then my beaming father gave him one of those manly hugs with a big slap on the back. My father's smile faded for a brief second, and then he slapped Rico on the back again.

"Good luck, son," he said. "Call if you need anything."

Rico stepped into his car. I waved as he rolled out of the driveway, and then jumped into a sprint towards him. I ran right up to his window. Rico slowed down and his deep brown eyes looked into mine.

"Hammer away," I said.

He looked at me, and smiled. I stepped away from his car. As I watched my brother drive down Broadway Ave., I thought of all the days he must have spent wondering if he would ever get another shot.

And finally, he had his chance.

About the Author

Instead of telling you about myself, I'd rather tell you a story about my friend, Kate. I call her Kate the Great. Here's why.

Kate joined a group of her friends for basketball lessons with me back in January of 1997. The other girls had been practicing for months, and they scored many baskets. Kate tried her best, but her shots didn't even reach the bottom of the net.

Despite her struggles, Kate returned to practice. For five weeks, she did not make a single shot. After a while, Kate was so nervous that she didn't even want to have the ball in her hands. One day in the middle of a lay-up drill, Kate started to cry. I took her aside and we practiced together for a few minutes. She rejoined the group, but still did not make a basket that day. I was sure Kate had to be thinking about quitting.

But she didn't. The next week Kate made 22 baskets in one hour. She looked more comfortable because she believed she could play basketball.

In June of that same year, I held a camp for the kids at Kate's school. All week, I had everyone keep track of their free throws. At the end of the week, I looked down my list and smiled. Kate was one of the top finishers. I announced to everyone that we would hold the championship in front of the entire camp, and then I read the list of finalists.

"If I called your name," I said, "start warming up."

As the others began to practice, Kate walked up to me with a frown. "Do we have to do this?" she asked.

I nodded my head, and Kate sighed. After doing so well, I didn't want Kate to doubt herself all over again. But then I realized that this was no longer a little game in front of her friends. This would be in front of all of her classmates.

"Are you scared to miss in front of everyone?" I asked.

Kate nodded.

"If you don't at least try, you will never know what you could have done," I told her.

Kate sighed again and turned away. She walked off to her basket, and started practicing.

The six finalists were shooting at three different baskets. I stood underneath Kate's basket and rebounded all five of her perfect swishes. Kate still looked nervous as she walked up to the main basket for the final round of free throws. I lined all the kids up on the stage to watch. The first player made two out of five shots. Then it was Kate's turn.

Kate stepped up to the line, nervously twisting her hands in her T-shirt. I passed her the ball and she dribbled it quickly. Her eyes grew wide as she looked up at the basket. The ball went up, and fell right through the net.

Kate missed the second, but she kept her focus. She made the third and missed the fourth. It came down to one last shot. The gym fell silent. Kate eyed the rim and let the ball go.

Swish!

Kate had won the free throw contest.

I love to tell that story and I always remind myself of what I learned from it. Just when I might consider the risk involved in publishing these books myself, I think about Kate the Great.

In your hands is my second book.

Be on the lookout for more books by

Ballplayers

Book # 3
Everybody's Favorite
by Penny

When Penny Harris finds out the Ballplayers have a chance to go to soccer camp, she can't wait. But there's only one catch — they have to raise all the money in one week. Along the way, the Ballplayers run into trouble, and everyone looks to one person to save the day. Will Penny be able to work everything out?

Available Now!

Book #4
Don't Stop
by Angel

Angel Russomano loves to run and play. In high school, the cross country season and the soccer season are in the fall, so Angel decides to play on both teams. But the true test for Angel is balancing her sports with the pressures at school and problems at home. Will Angel be strong enough?

Due out in Fall '98

Be a Ballplayer, too!

Join the
Ballplayer Book Club!

To find out more about **The Broadway Ballplayers**™, sign up to be on the mailing list. Send a slip of paper with your name and full address to:

The Broadway Ballplayers™
P.O. Box 597
Wilmette, IL 60091
(847)-570-4715

Drop a note to the kids from Broadway Ave. Maybe one of them will write back to you!

Check out our website at **www.bplayers.com**